THE UNIC🦄RN CLUB®

BOYFRIENDS FOR EVERYONE

Written by
Alice Nicole Johansson

Created by
FRANCINE PASCAL

BANTAM BOOKS
NEW YORK · TORONTO · LONDON · SYDNEY · AUCKLAND

To Jacqueline Marie Campo

RL 4, 008-012

BOYFRIENDS FOR EVERYONE
A Bantam Book / April 1997

Sweet Valley High® and The Unicorn Club®
are registered trademarks of Francine Pascal.

Conceived by Francine Pascal.

Produced by Daniel Weiss Associates, Inc.
33 West 17th Street
New York, NY 10011.

Cover art by Bruce Emmett.

ISBN: 0-553-48445-1
Published simultaneously in the United States and Canada

Bantam Books are published by Bantam Books, a division of Bantam
Doubleday Dell Publishing Group, Inc. Its trademark, consisting of the
words "Bantam Books" and the portrayal of a rooster, is Registered in U.S.
Patent and Trademark Office and in other countries. Marca Registrada.
Bantam Books, 1540 Broadway, New York, New York 10036.

PRINTED IN THE UNITED STATES OF AMERICA

OPM   0 9 8 7 6 5 4 3 2 1

One

*Ellen, I went shopping. You were still sleeping,
so I told the desk to hold all calls. Lila.*

Ellen Riteman removed the note that Lila Fowler had
left taped to the hotel mirror. She dropped it in the
fancy white faux marble plastic wastebasket with the
gold St. Maurice Caribbean Hostess Hotel crest.

"Mirror mirror on the wall, who's the fairest of
them all?" she sleepily asked her reflection.

"You are, Ellen Riteman," Ellen told herself, pretending to be the mirror. Then she giggled. "Hard
to believe, huh?"

Ellen reached over and flipped on the radio. She
was tired of talking to herself.

*"Pacific Rim mutual funds are showing some strong
growth potential,"* a dry-voiced announcer intoned.

"And if interest rates go down, the risk is still low because the investor is diversified. . . ."

Click!

"I'd rather talk to myself in the mirror," Ellen muttered. She flipped the switch until she found some light, romantic, Caribbean instrumental. "Ah. That's better."

Ellen swayed to the music and studied her reflection. She had to admit, she wasn't a bad-looking girl underneath her pink pimple cream and faded sleep shirt. But she was an unlikely candidate for Queen of the Caribbean Teen Cruise, the ten-day trip sponsored by *Dream Teen* magazine.

Ellen and her four best friends—Jessica Wakefield, Mandy Miller, Lila Fowler, and Kimberly Haver—had all decided to take the trip together.

The package included three days on a luxurious cruise ship, three days in this plush resort hotel on the island of St. Maurice, and then three more days on the ship.

They'd arrived at the hotel last night, and the girls had decided to duplicate the same sleeping arrangements they had on board the cruise ship: Ellen, Lila, and Lila's extensive (not to mention expensive) wardrobe in one room and Jessica, Kimberly, and Mandy across the hall in room 1415.

Ellen and her friends were all members of the Unicorn Club. They considered themselves the prettiest and most popular seventh and eighth graders at Sweet Valley Middle School.

It had been a bummer year for Ellen. Her parents had gotten a divorce, and things on the home front were kind of tense. Ellen had been looking forward to getting away from the stress and strain of joint custody and spending ten days with her four best friends.

But as soon as they got aboard the ship, her four best friends decided that what Ellen *really* needed to cheer her up was *male* company.

The Unicorns were a competitive bunch. When they started to compete for the "matchmaker of the cruise" title, Ellen's life turned complicated.

Jessica, playing Fairy Godmother number one, had produced Sam Sloane.

Lila, Fairy Godmother number two (the one with the gold credit card and the extensive, expensive wardrobe), had dubbed Jared Matthews the most eligible guy on board.

Mandy, Fairy Godmother number three, had insisted that only Jack could make Ellen happy.

And Kimberly, Fairy Godmother number four, had stubbornly backed her own choice, Peter.

Ellen had done her duty and romantically ensnared them all.

It hadn't been love at first sight or anything like that. No way. No, Ellen had to be a different princess for each prince. She had to change personalities (not to mention clothes and accessories) for every date.

It was hard work. But Ellen was turning out to be good at it.

She hadn't done it without help, though. Fairy

Godmothers one through four had rallied—producing clothes, makeup, tips on deportment, and appropriate conversational gambits for each guy.

Result?

She, Ellen Riteman, the girl most likely to finish last in virtually any competition, was now juggling the four cutest guys on the trip.

It was a pretty heavy load of guys to handle, no doubt. Ellen wished she could reduce the volume.

But the problem was, how did Ellen dump any of the guys from the lineup without offending one of her Fairy Godmothers (aka best friends)?

It would be, like, the ultimate insult to their taste.

So when the princes called, Ellen answered.

The little red light on the telephone blinked frantically. Messages!

Ellen picked up the phone and dialed the desk of the St. Maurice Caribbean Hostess Hotel.

"Concierge. Good morning. How may I assist you?" the concierge trilled into the phone in her French-accented English. The people on the island spoke French, though luckily for Ellen, everyone who worked at the hotel could speak English.

Ellen ran a hand through her tangled hair. "This is Cinderella, which prince called?"

"I beg your pardon?"

Ellen sat down on the edge of her bed. "Oh, excuse me. I forgot. This isn't Cinderella. This is Snow White. You know, it's so hard to keep these things straight when your life is one big fairy tale."

"Pardon?" the concierge repeated.

"Would you believe, Little Red Riding Hood?"

"Who is this?" the concierge pressed.

"I wish I knew," Ellen retorted.

"Mademoiselle is perhaps playing a joke?" the voice suggested irritably.

Mademoiselle is *a joke*, Ellen felt like answering, looking down at her pilled and matted fuzzy slippers and her faded sleep shirt. They didn't exactly match the decor of her luxurious hotel room. They didn't match her glammed-out popular girl image either.

Still, they gave her a sense of security. The slippers and sleep shirt had been a present from her parents last Christmas. The last Christmas before the divorce.

"Allo! Allo!" the impatient concierge yodeled, urging her to get to the point.

"This is Ellen Riteman in room 1414. Do I have any messages?"

"Just a moment," the voice said curtly. Ellen heard the *tap tap tap* of the desk computer. "Ah, *oui*. For Ms. Riteman. Jack called to remind you that you have a date to go walking after lunch. Jared called to remind you that you have a date with him for lunch. Peter called and would like you to call him as soon as possible. And Sam Sloane requests also that you call him as soon as possible."

"Thank you," Ellen said, feeling a slight throbbing sensation in the back of her head just above her neck.

So many guys. So little time.

Ellen opened the curtains and looked out over the beach, the ocean, and the crowded pool and patio area directly below her room. Even from the fourteenth floor of the luxury high-rise, she could hear the music thumping.

Her stomach rumbled hungrily. Was there any possibility that the complimentary continental breakfast was still available in the pool pavilion? If so, she wanted to get her fair share of muffins and juice. She needed to fortify herself. It was going to be a hectic day. The Multiple Personality Princess was going to need her strength.

Ellen turned away from the window and opened the closet. "Let's see," she mused, staring at the collection of borrowed dresses, bathing suits, party outfits, and shoes. "Who am I this morning?"

Jessica Wakefield took a sip of her Raspberry-Apricot-Fit-for-a-Princess-Frozen-Infusion drink and adjusted the back of her lounge chair so that she had a better view of the pool, the palms, and the glistening white beach that surrounded the St. Maurice Caribbean Hostess Hotel.

The four-star hotel's pool was shaped like a pair of dolphins and featured a built-in pool bar. From her lounge chair, Jessica could see Kimberly Haver swimming athletically toward the bar. Several guys and girls were gathered around it, sipping exotic drinks and bopping to the beat of the piped-in reggae music.

Kimberly ordered a drink, paid for it with some

of the plastic beads the hotel had given them to use instead of money, and climbed out of the pool. Her wet feet made an angry flapping sound on the pavement as she walked quickly through the crowd of guys and girls. Kimberly was into swimming. She had great muscle definition in her arms and legs and had a deep tan. But her face looked as if she had lost the most important race of her life—and the scowl on her face said, *P.S. don't expect me to be a good sport about it either.*

Normally, Jessica got annoyed with Kimberly when she acted like a grump. But this time, Kimberly's grumpiness was understandable. Jessica could definitely relate.

Jessica reached for her sunscreen, poured a little into the palm of her hand, and rubbed it leisurely around the complicated crisscrossed straps of her new pink swimsuit.

The suit was almost the same color as her exotic drink. She took a sip of the icy liquid and then replaced the cap on her sunscreen with a heavy sigh. "I've never been so miserable in my life," she announced, leaning back and adjusting her glasses and visor to keep the warm tropical sun off of her nose.

Kimberly adjusted the back of her lounge chair with an irritated squeak. "I thought this trip was going to be the most fantastic ten days of my life. And it's turning into a nonstop nightmare."

"Yoo-hoo! Ellen!" A tall girl named Anna Beardsley waved her hand at Ellen, who had just emerged from the bank of elevators that opened onto the outdoor area of the hotel.

The first floor of the hotel featured a connecting series of covered outdoor walkways. Shops and service desks lined the perimeter of the main outdoor lobby area. Coffee bars, restaurants, and cafés dotted the hotel complex.

Colorful tropical birds were free to come and go. It wasn't unusual to see them flying in and out of the lobby area and foraging for crumbs right inside the restaurants.

This morning, when the elevator had opened, Jessica had found herself face-to-face with very tall, very pink, and very bored flamingo.

The second-floor lobby was completely enclosed and was connected to an enormous main dining room. Above that floor were twenty more floors of rooms just like the one Jessica shared with Kimberly and Mandy.

Jessica squinted through her pink-rimmed sunglasses and watched Ellen walk slowly around the pool, waving to all her friends and admirers.

"Have lunch with us?" Anna invited, pointing to her brother, Tommy, and her friends Kickie Crookshank and Danny Orisman. They were the celebrities on the cruise. Tommy and Anna were the fabulously wealthy heirs to a large fortune. Kickie Crookshank was the youngest U.S. gold medal winner for diving. And Danny Orisman was the son of Hector Orisman, the famous director of

Teens in Tears, the incredibly romantic movie that had broken a lot of box office records.

Jessica would have loved to be able to say they were her friends, but she only knew them through Ellen, who had been lucky enough to faint dead away at a private dinner party in the cruise ship captain's dining room. Ever since, Anna, Tommy, Danny, and Kickie acted like Ellen was their very best friend in the world and totally fragile. It was really sickening.

"Say you will," Kickie begged.

Ellen fluttered her fingers. "I'm not sure what my schedule is. Can I let you know?"

"Well, I guess. But don't get too tired," Kickie cautioned. "We don't want you fainting from exhaustion again."

"Ha ha ha ha!" Ellen laughed lightly, continuing on toward the pool pavilion where the breakfast buffet was served.

"Ha ha ha ha," Kimberly mimicked under her breath.

Jessica watched Ellen wave to a group of seventh-grade girls from Anaheim and four guys from San Diego, who one by one had danced with Ellen at the welcome party last night in the ballroom— while Jessica, Kimberly, Lila, and Mandy had sat around like a bunch of wallflowers.

"I liked Ellen better when she was insecure and didn't have any friends besides us," Kimberly grumbled. She threw herself moodily into the lounge chair, picked up a magazine, and loudly flipped the pages. "I refuse to watch Ms. Popularity work the crowd."

"I can't stop," Jessica responded. "It's like a car wreck. You hate yourself for watching, but you can't help yourself." She finished her drink with a thoughtful slurp.

Jessica watched Ellen make her way slowly toward the pool pavilion. Every few feet, she stopped to talk to someone.

It was, like, so weird.

Jessica wasn't conceited or anything like that, but she couldn't figure out why no one was paying *her*—or the other Unicorns, for that matter—that kind of attention. Back in Sweet Valley, people were always telling Jessica that she looked like a beauty queen with her blond, California girl good looks and her upbeat, California girl personality.

Kimberly Haver was very pretty too. And incredibly athletic. She also had a take-charge attitude that usually helped her get what she wanted.

Jessica didn't have one bad thing to say about Mandy Miller. Mandy was artistic and creative. And she was nice to everybody.

As for Jessica's best friend, Lila Fowler, she was the richest girl in Sweet Valley. Lila was spoiled and could be a real snob, but she had a wardrobe fit for a queen and lived with her father in a gorgeous mansion, where she threw incredibly lavish parties. That won her a lot of points around Sweet Valley Middle School.

Jessica had to admit that Kimberly, Mandy, and Lila could probably give her a run for her money in a popularity contest.

But the one girl who Jessica would have thought had NO chance whatsoever of dusting her—or Mandy or Lila or Kimberly—was the president of the Unicorn Club herself, Ellen Riteman.

Ellen was pretty. And she was funny. But she was incredibly insecure and a major space cadet. It wasn't so much that she *couldn't* compete with the other girls; it was that she was such a goofball, she'd never get it together on her own to try.

From day one of the trip, it had been clear to Jessica that Ellen was going to be a problem. Ellen's idea of a dream vacation was for the five of them to all hang out together like they were on some big floating mall.

Jessica and the others wanted to meet guys and have a fabulous romantic ten days. Not hang out in a girl pack.

Things got even worse when Curtis Bowman came along and attached himself to Ellen like a barnacle.

Jessica wanted Ellen to have a guy of her own—but not a phony baloney surfer wanna-be like Curtis Bowman. After all, if one Unicorn had a below par guy, it made the whole club look bad.

Jessica had seen from the get go that the only way to one, salvage the honor of the club, and two, have ten days of romance in the sun with some great guy was to one, detach Ellen from Curtis

Bowman and two, get her a guy who was up to Unicorn standards.

And so the Unicorns had searched for superior male specimens and presented them for Ellen's inspection. Jessica's pick was Sam Sloane—the greatest guy she had ever met. Unfortunately, by the time Jessica realized that she was madly in love with Sam Sloane, Sam was madly in love with Ellen Riteman.

Mandy Miller walked along the beach, scouting shells and trying to pretend she didn't see the couples that walked past her hand in hand. Most of them were from the teen cruise.

The surf boomed against the pier several yards down, and she jumped. Mandy reached back and massaged the bunched muscles in her neck.

This Ellen situation was really making her tense. Mandy didn't want to be catty or mean, but how could she help feeling catty and mean? She had dressed Ellen Riteman in her own clothes and coached her on how to seem artistic so that she could impress Jack.

Jack was impressed. And now Mandy was *de*-pressed.

How could she have been so stupid as to hand over her personality, her fashion sense, her artistic thoughts, and the greatest guy in the whole world to Ellen?

Mandy sat on a dune and spread out her collection of shells. A chip of iridescent abalone would make a great earring. The tiny clamshells with the holes could be strung with some thread and made into a necklace. If she found enough shells, she could wear it tonight.

Mandy looked up and squinted. A familiar figure was moving toward her. Jack! His shoulder-length brown hair blew back behind him, and his loose black pants and T-shirt billowed romantically.

And for once, he didn't have Ellen hanging on his arm.

Mandy waved. Maybe with Ellen safely out of the way, they could actually have an intelligent conversation.

Jack was an artist and a poet. And he also inspired Mandy to write a poem.

Jack is a dark silhouette against the sun. Bright around the edges and an eternal mystery.

Mandy had written that last night on a napkin during the dance—while she watched him dance with Ellen. She had stuffed it into the pocket of her jacket—which she'd lent Ellen in the morning. She wondered if Ellen had found the poem.

"Hi," Jack said, smiling as he sat down beside her.

"Hi," she said, smiling back. "Just taking a walk."

Jack looked out across the water. "I'm thinking of a poem. For someone very special." His large, expressive eyes met hers. "Mandy," he began in a soft tone.

Her heart beat a little faster. How could she have doubted him? Jack was artistic and sensitive and intuitive. He knew. He knew that it was Mandy who was artistic and sensitive. Not Ellen. She gazed at him. "Yes?" Mandy asked breathlessly.

Jack leaned a little closer. Fine grains of sand sparkled like glitter in his dark brows. "I want to ask you something."

"You can ask me anything," she said quietly.

He put one hand over hers and traced the line of her fingernail. "Can you think of anything that rhymes with *Ellen? Besides Magellan?*"

Two

How long can I keep this act up? Ellen wasn't sure she had the stamina it took to be this popular. All she'd done was walk from the lobby to the pool pavilion and back to the lobby. It had taken her thirty minutes because she'd had to stop twelve times to talk to people.

Maybe I'll take a nap. She'd just awakened, but the idea of having to be popular all day long made her feel sleepy all over again.

Ellen quickened her step. She'd get back in the bed with her muffins and juice, put on her sleep shirt again, and instruct the concierge to pull up the draw-bridge and tell the princes to go jump in the moat.

The lobby was only a few yards away. With any luck, she could get to the elevator and up to her room without . . .

"Ellen! Wait for me."

Her heart sank. She recognized Peter's voice immediately. Mr. Healthy Mind Healthy Body. Kimberly's selection for Perfect Guy for Ellen. "Hi, Peter."

He had obviously just come from the tennis court, and his white shirt and shorts were soaked with sweat. "Good workout. I called your room to see if you wanted to play a set, but I didn't get any answer. Did you go to the morning yoga class?"

As if, Ellen thought. "Oh, yes," she lied.

"Think you could handle two yoga classes in one day?" he asked with a smile. "There's a group leaving for a two-mile hike to the top of Mt. Maurice late this afternoon. They're going to conduct an evening yoga class on the mountaintop before dinner. It's a great way to center your mind and body at the end of the day. Want to go together?"

"Well . . . " Ellen caught a glimpse of Jessica and Kimberly sitting in lounge chairs by the pool. Kimberly was glaring at her over the top of her magazine. Ellen bit her lip. Kimberly was so touchy these days. The least little thing seemed to irritate her. If it would make Kimberly happy for Ellen to go with Peter, then Ellen would do it, even if it killed her. "I'd love to," she said quickly.

"I'll meet you at the gate." Peter grinned, tapped his heel with his racket, and hurried away.

Ellen continued on, smothering a yawn. Her head was really starting to hurt. Nobody ever wanted to be a wallflower—but after last night,

Ellen had decided that being a wallflower was really underrated. Her feet were killing her. Dancing in Lila's expensive pumps had left blisters on both big toes. And she was going to have to wear them again tonight, because Jared had invited her to go dancing at a very private disco.

Just thinking about it made her big-toe knuckles throb. She yawned again. Was there any way she could get out of it? No way could she make the hike and then go dancing.

"What's the matter, party girl? Too much fun gettin' yeeeeeoooo down."

Ellen smiled, recognizing Curtis Bowman's heavy California accent.

"Hi, Curtis," she said. Curtis stood at the elevators, wearing long, baggy Hawaiian shorts. His long blond hair hung dripping around his shoulders.

"I didn't see you in the pool," she said.

"I wasn't in the pool." Curtis grinned. "Why would anybody swim in a pool when there's an ocean out there?"

"It's kind of rough out there, isn't it?" Ellen asked.

Curtis smiled. "Yeah!" He pushed his wet hair back and met her eyes. "Wanna go out with me? Out in the water, I mean? Surfing?" Curtis's blue eyes were hopeful and friendly. "Bodysurfing," he added quickly. "You wouldn't need a board or anything. We could get some junk food and sodas and have a picnic too."

Ellen felt a little flutter in her stomach, followed by a pang of guilt. She couldn't help getting flutters when he smiled at her. But then she felt guilty, because she knew her friends totally disapproved of him. They thought he was a dork and a phony. A surfer wanna-be. They called him *Surfer Dude*.

Still, Ellen thought he was cute. And he was nice. And he liked her for herself—whoever that was. She was a little confused at this point. But she figured that maybe a junk food picnic and swim would clear her mind. "I'd really love to," Ellen told him.

"He's asking her out," Kimberly said through clenched teeth.

"Say yes," Jessica urged under her breath. "Yes. Yes. Yes." She began smoothing sunscreen on her legs. The bottle made a gloopy empty sound, and Jessica whacked the bottom of it. A large splat of sunscreen came out and hit Kimberly's magazine. Kimberly let out a gasp of irritation and slapped at the smeared pages with the edge of her towel.

Whack!
Splat!
Slap! Slap!
Gee, don't worry about trying to be subtle, Ellen thought, beginning to feel annoyed with Fairy Godmothers numbers one and four. Good grief! Why didn't Jessica and Kimberly just jump up, wave their arms, and scream, *"Oooooga! Oooooga!"*?

"Gosh! I'd love to," Ellen said a little louder,

hoping her voice would carry. "But I just don't see how I can work it in."

Curtis continued smiling, but something left his face. "Yeah. Well, uh, I know you've got a lot of dudes, so . . . maybe some other time." He bobbed his head good-bye and sidled off, cutting through the leafy fronds of the thick hedge to get to the beach.

Ellen hoped the other Unicorns had heard her brush Curtis off. She hated to do it, but her friendships with Jessica, Mandy, Lila, and Kimberly were too important to risk over Curtis Bowman, the wanna-be surfer dude.

Her eyes lingered on the palm fronds, hoping against hope that just maybe Curtis wasn't the type to give up that easily.

Behind the potted palm, Lila gritted her teeth and fought the impulse to stamp her foot. She ducked back into the gift shop and lingered in front of the racks of cosmetics.

"Why did we *ever* talk her out of going out with Curtis Bowman?" she muttered to herself. A lump rose in her throat. Ellen Riteman was having the time of her life, while she, Lila Fowler, was having the worst time of her life. It wasn't fair.

What had made Lila think that only someone like Jared Matthews would be good enough for Ellen?

Anybody was good enough for Ellen. Even Curtis Bowman. It wasn't like Ellen was anybody important—despite what Lila had told Jared Matthews.

I was insane, Lila thought angrily. *Out of my mind. Delusional from the sun.* When Lila had spotted Jared flashing his gold charge card around the gift shop on the ship, she'd made up her mind that he would be perfect for Ellen.

So she'd made up a story about Ellen. She had told Jared that Ellen was one of the "California Ritemans," an eccentric, aristocratic descendant of the Royal Family of Sabolaslavichnia.

Ellen wasn't good enough for Jared, Lila realized now. Jared was special. Sure, he was handsome, rich, and a snob. But he wasn't superficial. Just right for Lila.

"Hi there! You're just the person I've been looking for."

Lila gasped when Jared came strolling around the corner of the candy rack. Maybe somebody had clued him in. Told him the truth. Told him that Ellen was a nobody and Lila was a somebody. "Why were you looking for me?" she asked, giving him her most flirtatious smile.

"I wanted you to help me pick out something for Ellen. Do you know what kind of candy she likes?"

"Oh, Ellen probably shouldn't have any candy," Lila said quickly.

Jared frowned. "Why not?"

"Well, you know how girls like that are," Lila replied breezily.

"Like what?"

"A little heavy," Lila whispered.

Jared's eyes flashed. "Ellen isn't heavy."

"Maybe *heavy* is the wrong word," Lila amended quickly. "But . . . well . . . she does worry about her complexion."

"Ellen's complexion is beautiful," Jared insisted.

"Well . . . sure . . . because she works at it and doesn't eat a lot of candy."

Jared studied Lila skeptically.

Lila decided it was probably better not to let him think about it too long. She smiled sweetly and took his arm. She steered him over to the magazine rack. "Look. Why don't you get her that special edition of *Big Bucks* magazine. The one on mutual funds." Lila snatched the magazine from the shelf and thrust it into his hands.

Jared stared at it blankly, then fanned the pages. "Does Ellen know about stuff like mutual funds?"

Lila nodded. "Oh, yes. In fact, Ellen is in charge of all her own investments."

Jared examined the back cover with a frown. "Ellen is only in the seventh grade."

"Sure. But she's a financial wizard. I'm sure that a magazine on mutual funds would be exactly the right gift," Lila insisted.

Jared's eyes wandered toward the candy rack where beautiful boxes of foil-wrapped chocolates were prominently displayed.

"You're sure?" he asked nervously. "I mean, she wouldn't think it was too dry or unromantic?"

"No way." Lila smiled inwardly and walked

him toward the cash register. *Away* from the candy rack *and* the stuffed animals *and* the attractive native crafts *and* the jewelry and everything else that Ellen might have enjoyed receiving as a gift.

So far, Lila was the only Unicorn with the guts to actually fight back. When Ellen had gone with Jared to dine in the Captain's private dining room, Lila had sawed halfway through the red high heels she had lent Ellen to wear.

She'd been sure that Ellen would fall, make a total fool out of herself, and disgust Jared completely.

Unfortunately, Ellen had fainted from exhaustion before she'd had a chance to wipe out. She had been rushed to the ship's infirmary to recuperate. The red dress and shoes were probably still there. Lila made a note to collect her designer silk dress before the end of the trip.

Plan Red Shoes had failed. Plan Mutual Funds was more subtle, but would probably be more effective; Lila was pretty sure it could work. The minute Jared presented Ellen with a magazine on mutual funds, a series of things would happen. Ellen would get that confused, dumb look on her face that drove her friends crazy. Jared would expect her to say something intelligent on the subject of mutual funds. Ellen would think any guy who would give her a present like that would have to be the thickest, most unromantic guy in the world. Mutual disenchantment would be inevitable.

Yep. Lila felt pretty sure that by tonight, Jared

would be free and fall into her own waiting arms.

As Jared paid for the magazine, something caught Lila's eye. "I'll see you later," she said happily to Jared.

He nodded. "See you later."

Lila left the gift shop and took a right, heading for the dress boutique. There was a floral-print wrap skirt in the window that would be just right for walking in the moonlight with Jared Matthews.

A hand darted out from behind a pot full of red and yellow blooms and closed over Lila's arm.

"Hey!" she cried.

"Shhhh!" Jessica warned, pulling Lila into a narrow walkway that housed a large air-conditioning unit and ice machine. Kimberly lurked behind the ice machine, keeping watch.

"What's going on?" Lila demanded angrily, brushing off the sleeve of her expensive silk blouse. "I thought I was being mugged."

"We don't want Ellen to see us," Jessica explained. "It's time for a meeting. An emergency session of the Unicorns."

"What about?" Lila asked.

"What do you mean what about?" Kimberly demanded. "What else? The Ellen problem, that's what."

"I don't have a problem with Ellen," Lila said smugly.

Jessica frowned in confusion. "What do you mean?"

"I mean I'm taking steps to protect my interests."

"Oh, yeah!" Kimberly said. "Then what's happening over there?"

The three girls all turned and saw Jared talking with Ellen by the palm. Ellen was tossing her head and laughing. "A mutual funds magazine. Oh Jared! What a great present. You know, those Pacific Rim funds are really showing some growth potential."

"What did she say?" Jessica whispered.

"And if interest rates go down, your risk is still low because you're so diversified," Ellen continued enthusiastically.

"Where is she *getting* that stuff?" Lila felt her face growing pale. "Ellen doesn't know anything about mutual funds."

"No. But her mom is studying for her real estate license and is really into learning about business," Kimberly said. "I guess she's just parroting her opinions. That seems to be the one thing Ellen can do really well."

"Let's talk about it over lunch," Jared suggested. "Maybe you can explain it to me."

"Oh, no," Ellen said, stuffing the magazine down into her bag. "I'm sure we can find other things to talk about." They laughed. An intimate, knowing laugh that made Lila's hair stand on end.

She turned to her friends, her mouth in a line. "What time is the meeting?" she whispered fiercely.

Three

"We never should have tried to help Ellen," Lila groaned, flopping across Kimberly's bed. "We tried to help her find a guy and we created a monster. A man-eating monster."

Mandy sat down on the end of her bed cross-legged. Her friends had just arrived in her room for an emergency Unicorn meeting. "Look. We all contributed to this situation and we're all going to have to work together to correct it."

Jessica sighed heavily. "What do you suggest? We can't exactly tell Ellen to quit showing us up. We do have some pride, you know."

Mandy cupped her chin in her hand. "She's got to be made to understand that we don't like what she's doing. That she's gotten way too impressed with herself. Ellen really wants us all to be friends, right? If we give her the cold shoulder for a while, she'll get the message and straighten up."

"Mandy's right," Lila agreed. "That'll show her. It'll be a very clear message that we made her and we can break her just as easily."

Mandy took a deep breath. "Lila, leave Ellen a note. Tell her we're all going to get together this afternoon for coffee after lunch. We'll all talk, laugh, and leave her completely out of the conversation. She'll clue in."

Mandy's heart gave a guilty little thump. She didn't enjoy treating anyone so coldly. But this was war.

"Ha ha ha ha ha!" Jessica threw back her head and roared with laughter, pounding the table. She was sitting in Café Misto with Lila, Kimberly, and Mandy. Ellen had just walked into the door. "Kimberly, you are sooooo funny."

Ellen appeared at the table dressed in one of Lila's most expensive dresses—a green silk slip dress with a double-breasted white linen jacquard jacket. She slid into the booth beside Jessica. "What's so funny?" she asked with a smile.

Jessica let her laugh die down to a chuckle. "Oh," she said evasively, "you had to be there." She turned away from Ellen. "So Kimberly, did you check out what time the band starts tonight?"

Kimberly sat forward. "You guys, we are going to have the best time tonight."

"What are we going to do?" Ellen asked eagerly.

Kimberly froze, as if she had just revealed something that was supposed to be a secret.

"You wouldn't be interested," Jessica said abruptly.

Ellen's face fell a fraction. Jessica smiled inwardly and leaned forward, deliberately turning her head so that she faced away from Ellen, and began to talk to Lila in a whisper.

Ellen's heart sank deeper and deeper into her stomach as her friends chatted and laughed. They were giving her the arctically cold shoulder.

Ellen knew why too. It was because of Curtis. Kimberly and Jessica had seen her talking to Curtis this morning and had told the others. Now they were angry at her.

Jessica, Mandy, Lila, and Kimberly had selflessly dedicated themselves to Ellen's happiness. And Ellen had acted like an ingrate. Actually thinking of herself as a victim of the wonderful gift they had given her—popularity.

They had worked really really hard to mold her looks and personality so she would be a big success with guys. But they had guessed that she was just going through the motions and not really putting her heart into it.

Ellen bit her lip, determined not to cry. She was going to double her efforts to impress the guys if that's what it took to make her friends happy. She would read that mutual funds magazine from cover to cover. She would actually pretend that gaggy poem Mandy scripted for her and tucked into the pocket of her jacket was something she had written for Jack. She would go on a two-mile hike with Peter. And she would dance the night away with Jared.

She would make sure that her friends knew she was trying. She couldn't just keep taking, taking, taking without giving something back.

Four

An hour after the girls left the coffee bar, Mandy went back to the beach and lay on her stomach, staring gloomily out over the ocean.

She felt pretty small right now. She had an impulse to apologize to Ellen. But with any luck, that wouldn't be necessary. Ellen would get the message and back off.

Mandy heard a seagull cawing overhead and turned over, hoping to watch it swoop gracefully through the sky. Where was it? She put her hand up to shield her eyes from the glare. No seagull circled above. So where was that cawing coming from?

Mandy's stomach clenced. She realized that the noise wasn't a seagull's caw at all—but Ellen's laugh. Mixed with a deeper, melodious laugh—*Jack's!*

In spite of herself, Mandy turned to look.

Ellen and Jack came running along the beach, hand in hand.

Ellen saw Mandy and waved, pulling on Jack's hand. A few moments later, they flopped down beside Mandy.

"Jack wrote a poem for me," Ellen said, giving Jack the gooniest look Mandy had ever seen.

"Oh, really?" Mandy said politely.

"And to thank me, Ellen wrote a poem for *me*," Jack confided in a pleased tone.

Mandy raised her eyebrows. "Oh?"

Jack tore his eyes away from Ellen and fixed his gaze on the horizon line. He cleared his throat and began reciting: "'*Jack is a dark silhouette against the sun. Bright around the edges and an eternal mystery.*'"

Mandy wanted to scream. She couldn't believe it. Ellen. Ellen Riteman, Ms. Insecurity herself, had turned into the most duplicitous, double-dealing, poetry-stealing, man-hogging femme fatale in the Unicorn Club. And that was saying something.

And Jack had, like, no concept at all.

Mandy curled her toes so hard, she pulled the toe-piece of her rubber thong out of the sole. She wasn't taking this one lying down. It was time to fight back.

"*Jack is a dark silhouette against the sun. Bright around the edges and an eternal mystery,*" Mandy repeated in a musing tone. "I don't know. I have to be honest. It just doesn't sound like much of a poem. I mean, it's not very long."

"It's a haiku," Ellen said in an *explaining* tone of voice that made Mandy want to push her face in the sand.

"A haiku? Really?" Mandy forced herself to sound pleasant. "And how, exactly, would you define a haiku?" she asked.

Ellen looked taken aback for a moment, then she fluttered her eyelashes and looked upward, as if she were searching for the right words. "I'm not sure I can really *define* haiku," she said thoughtfully.

Exactly, Mandy thought triumphantly.

Jack stared at the shore. "I'm trying to think of a way to define haiku," he said after a moment. "Ellen could probably put it better than I can, but I think a haiku is usually characterized by short, elegant, and very descriptive phrases." He shot a look at Ellen, as if eager for her input.

Ellen rolled her eyes upward and fluttered her eyelashes again. After a dramatic pause, she nodded. "Yes. I think that sums it up." She smiled at Mandy. "Does that help you at all?"

Ellen ran beside Jack, trying to be graceful. They had left Mandy and were on their way to do some sandpainting. In music videos, women never clenched their fists and pumped their arms when they ran along a beach. Their arms hung loose and sort of swayed around their bodies.

Ellen's arms refused to sway. They swung like dead weights instead, whapping her thighs. She felt totally dumb. But now that she had started running that way, she didn't know how to *stop* running that way without calling attention to it.

Short, elegant, descriptive phrases, huh?

Ellen moves like a bird. A big clumsy turkey, to be exact.

Or how about . . .

Sandpainting. Boring with a capital B.

If she hadn't been sure that Mandy's feelings would be hurt, Ellen would drop Jack like a hot potato.

The last thing in the world she felt like doing was messing around with a bunch of sand. Oh, well. She ought to be able to wrap up the sandpainting thing in less than an hour.

Actually, she had no choice.

She was due to meet Peter in an hour and a half.

"Gin," Kimberly announced, spreading out her cards.

Anna Beardsley peered at the cards, moving her lips as she counted. "You're right," she grudgingly admitted.

"Of course," her brother, Tommy, agreed, smiling at Kimberly. "She's won five hands in a row."

Kimberly did her best to smile. Tommy had invited her to join him and Anna in a game of cards at a table by the pool. Kimberly wasn't all that interested in the game—but sitting by the pool, she knew the chances were pretty good she'd see Peter.

A familiar male laugh behind her made her sit up straighter and fluff her hair a little. *Here he comes,* she thought happily.

"Ellen!" Anna cried, waving her hand. "Over here!"

The next thing Kimberly knew, Ellen was standing above her, holding on to Peter's hand like a ski rope.

Peter smiled at Kimberly. "Playing cards? Shame on you for sitting around on this gorgeous day."

"Oh, Kimberly's a great big slug just like us," Tommy said with a deep laugh.

Kimberly felt her face flush with anger and embarrassment. "No I'm not," she protested.

"Now, now," Anna chided, snickering. "We suggested parasailing, swimming, and hiking, and you said it was too hot and you were too tired."

"I'm exercising my mind," Kimberly managed to retort. "It's all about balance, remember. I exercised my body this morning in the pool, and now I'm exercising my brain."

"I don't think we gave her much exercise," Anna said with a wink. "She beat us five hands in a row."

"What are you playing?" Peter asked.

"Gin rummy," Tommy answered.

Peter laughed. "That's practically a kids' game. Ever played bridge? Now *that's* a challenging game."

"I love bridge," Kimberly said eagerly. She

wanted Peter to know she was no slouch, physically *or* mentally.

"So do I," Tommy said. "Ellen, I'll bet you play bridge. Maybe the four of us could play. Kimberly and me against you and Peter."

"That's a great idea!" Kimberly watched Ellen with narrowed eyes. Go Fish taxed Ellen's attention span. She was going to have to admit she didn't know how to play bridge.

Ellen looked at her watch and made a disappointed face. "Oh, I am sooooo sorry. But I don't have time. I haven't had any time to meditate today. If I don't do it now, I'll be a crank all evening."

Peter's face grew very respectful. "Oh, wow. Sure, I understand. It's important to keep yourself centered."

"We could still have a foursome," Anna suggested. "I'll take Ellen's place."

"No, thanks," Peter said, giving them a wave. "I'll go to my room and meditate too." He watched Ellen walk away. "Wow! She's a really great example. No matter what, she makes time for herself. That's so healthy."

Kimberly wondered if anybody else could see the steam coming out of her ears.

Ellen stepped into her room, shut the door behind her, and practically collapsed. Two miles! The guy was a sadist. In a just world, he would be locked up. Peter was a danger to himself and to the community—Ellen in particular.

She had to get rid of him.

Somehow.

Even if Kimberly never spoke to her again.

Not only was Peter an exercise fanatic, he talked constantly. The guy had more information than an encyclopedia. And he was determined to share every shred of it with Ellen.

On the dresser, there was an envelope of photos. Some of Lila's photographs were back from the developer.

Ellen couldn't resist taking a peek. She opened up the envelope and removed the stack of shiny photos. Most of them were taken on the day they left for the cruise.

There they all were, standing in front of Lila's dad's limousine—arms around each other and smiling. Kimberly was holding her fingers up behind Ellen's head in a V, like bunny ears, and laughing.

Ellen bit her lip. Kimberly could be a real grump sometimes. But when she was in a good mood, she was fun. And funny. A good friend too. How could Ellen do anything that would hurt Kimberly's feelings or make her angry? Even if Peter killed her with exercise and bored her to tears.

Jessica turned over in her lounge chair by the pool and stared at the pavement. She hadn't been able to hear the conversation between Ellen and Peter and Kimberly and the Beardsley twins, but she was dying to know what Ellen had said.

Unfortunately, Kimberly was still playing cards with Anna and Tommy. Jessica couldn't exactly go over and ask in front of them. A beach ball bounced off Jessica's back, and she sat up with gasp of irritation. She swallowed the gasp when she saw who had thrown the ball—Sam Sloane.

He was in the pool and grinning at her. "Sorry about that. Believe it or not, I really didn't mean to hit you."

Jessica couldn't help smiling back. Sam Sloane had the brightest smile she had ever seen on a guy. He had the widest shoulders too.

Sam put his hands on the edge of the pool and pulled himself out of the water with muscular grace. "Well, I did owe you one."

Jessica laughed, remembering how they had met. She had gone barging in the out door of the ship's game arcade as Sam was coming out. The door had whacked him in the nose. It hadn't done any damage. In fact, it had been the start of a beautiful friendship—between Sam and Ellen Riteman.

Jessica fought off a stab of jealousy. Ellen was pretty dense, but they'd done a good job of giving her the freeze this afternoon. Maybe she would take her phony fingernails out of Sam now.

Sam sat down in the empty chair beside Jessica. "This hotel is way fantastic. I've had the greatest day of my life. I went parasailing. It was totally awesome."

Jessica watched Sam's face and felt her heart

beat faster. Most guys would have sounded totally corny or phony acting that enthusiastic. But not Sam. He was genuinely interested in everything and everybody.

"Where's Ellen?" he asked. "I haven't seen her all day and I left a message for her this morning. I was hoping to get her to go parasailing with me."

Jessica settled herself in her lounge chair and pushed her sunglasses up on her nose. She had been waiting for the chance to drive a little wedge between Sam and Ellen, and Sam had just given her the opening she needed. "Well, you know Ellen has a lot of guys on the string," she said. "She's pretty busy most days."

Jessica shot a look at Sam, gauging the effect of her revelation.

Sam laughed and pushed his wet hair back off of his tanned, wide brow. "No lie," he agreed. "I'm just glad for whatever time I get with her. I like a girl who knows how to flirt and have fun with a lot of people." He looked fixedly at Jessica. "I'm that kind of person myself."

Jessica's heart began to thunder. He was speaking to *her* now—she was sure of it. He was telling her he was flirting with her, and that he wanted her to flirt back.

"Jessica," he said softly.

"Yes, Sam." Her voice was little more than a whisper.

"May I have the ball?"

She realized that she was still holding the multicolored beach ball. "Uh—sure," she responded uncertainly.

Sam put his hands on the ball but didn't pull the ball away. He seemed content to sit there, staring into Jessica's eyes. He leaned forward . . . closer . . .

Jessica's eyelids fluttered closed. He was going to kiss her. Sam Sloane was actually going to kiss her. She tried to relax her mouth. She'd been kissed before, but never by a guy like Sam.

"Yoo-hoo!" a voice yodeled behind her.

Jessica's eyes flew open. Sam was so startled by the noise, he jerked his head away and fell backward off of his lounge chair. "Whoaaaa!" he yelled.

"Oh, wow!" Ellen cried, hurrying over to help Sam up. "Are you OK? is anything broken?" Ellen was wearing a new bathing suit covered with smiley faces. Jessica thought she might cry. Ellen seemed to have absolutely no concept at all that she had just ruined everything.

Sam sat up, laughing. "Why is it that every time I get near you girls, I wind up getting knocked off my feet?" He pulled Ellen down next to him. "Or maybe I should say swept off my feet. Ellen, you look great in that suit. I *love* those smiley faces."

Ellen gave Jessica and Sam a bright smile. "I like clothes that make a statement. And when I feel happy, I like everybody to know it."

"Me too," Sam said in an enthusiastic tone. He reached for the beach ball and tossed it in the water. "Come on, Ellen. Let's play water polo."

"Oh I *love* water polo," Ellen squealed happily, jumping up and following Sam to the edge of the pool.

Jessica wished her leg were about two feet longer. That way she could reach out and kick Ellen right in the rear.

"Hello, Ms. Haver," Captain Jackson, the captain of the cruise ship, walked toward where Kimberly was standing outside the pro shop. Tommy and Anna Beardsley had gone upstairs for a rest, and Kimberly had spent some time looking at sports equipment.

"Hi," Kimberly replied, a little surprised to see him. "What are you doing here? I mean, if you're here, who's minding the ship?"

Captain Jackson smiled distantly. "I have a very competent first mate. I'm just here to have a meeting with the hotel manager and island Rescue Patrol. There's the possibility of a tropical storm and we have to coordinate our efforts."

"Hello, Captain Jackson." Jared Matthews came out of the pro shop and joined them. "Did I hear you say we may be in for a storm?"

Captain Jackson nodded and pointed at some black clouds gathering in the sky.

"A storm?" Kimberly frowned. "You mean like . . . a hurricane?"

"Well, it is that season," Captain Jackson said, "but I doubt we'll have anything that dramatic. Small watercraft have been advised to remain in port. And the planes and helicopters are grounded. But it's really just a precaution at this point. We may not have any kind of storm at all." He held out a bag. "When Ms. Riteman was taken ill in my dining room, her shoes were left behind. May I give these to you to return to her?"

Just hearing the word *Ellen* made Kimberly cringe. She knew, of course, that the shoes really belonged to Lila, but she wasn't in the mood to do either one of them a favor. "Well, it really wouldn't be convenient for me to take them right now," she said. "I'm going to take a walk."

"I'll take them," Jared said quickly. He took the bag from Captain Jackson. "I'm seeing Ellen this evening and I'll give them to her then."

"Very well," Captain Jackson said. He nodded briskly to Kimberly and Jared and then walked toward a group of uniformed officials standing near the entrance to the hotel manager's office.

Kimberly watched Jared strut down the hall, bag in hand. So Ellen hadn't blown him off either. From the looks of things, she was still milking her popularity for what it was worth.

Kimberly peered out the window. There was indeed a storm brewing, but it wasn't in the sky. It was right here in the hotel.

It was time for another meeting of the Unicorn Club.

"Project Cold Shoulder is officially scuttled," Jessica announced that night. "It was a total failure."

"Failure doesn't even begin to cover it," Kimberly fumed, pacing the length of the room she shared with Mandy and Jessica.

The girls were gathered for another meeting. Mandy lay facedown on the bed with her chin cupped in her hand. Lila sat on the edge of the bed with her arms folded across her chest and her foot tapping impatiently. And Jessica sat next to her with one leg curled beneath her and the other dangling over the edge. She chewed nervously at a ragged cuticle and watched Kimberly pace back and forth.

"Project Cold Shoulder just made Ellen worse." Kimberly threw her arms in the air. "I guess we made her mad, and she was determined to show us who was boss. Her. She was flaunting her popularity. Rubbing it in my face. Meditate! Ellen? Hah!"

Lila massaged her temple. "I feel like just packing it in and going home."

"You can't," Kimberly muttered.

"Why not?" Lila demanded.

"There's a tropical storm brewing," Kimberly explained. "No boats are leaving the island, and the planes and helicopters are grounded."

Lila, Mandy, and Jessica all let out a groan.

Kimberly stood again and put her hands on her hips. Her fellow Unicorns were sounding dangerously like losers. Ellen had psyched them all out. They had to snap out of it. And they had to snap out of it fast. "Right now, bad weather is the least of our problems," she reminded them. "Our number one vacation glitch is Ellen. And I think we've reached the point where we have to take drastic action."

Jessica stared at Kimberly with big, worried eyes. "Meaning?"

"Meaning we are not going to lay down and die." Kimberly looked around the room, making eye contact with each of her friends in turn. "We're not licked yet. We can still win. But we're going to have to use the deadliest weapon of them all."

"Which is?" Lila wanted to know.

Kimberly looked at her intently. *"The truth!"*

Five

"Wow! The wind is really blowing," Jared commented.

Ellen nodded. They had just left the private disco at the end of the beach and were walking hand in hand over the sand toward the hotel in the moonlight. Of all her personalities, Ellen found the rich, eccentric Ellen Riteman of the California Ritemans the hardest to maintain. It was the role that took the most physical stamina.

Lila had told Jared that Ellen had the hereditary Riteman tic. Which meant that every twenty minutes or so, Ellen had to open her mouth as wide as she could and yank her elbow up.

It actually fit in quite well at the disco, where people were flapping elbows in every direction. But she tended to forget about it when she was off the dance floor.

She glanced at her watch. Oops. Tic time. Ellen

opened her mouth wide and jerked her elbow up.

"Oommmph!" Jared groaned.

Ellen pretended not to notice that she had just elbowed Jared in the ribs—for the third time that evening.

He pretended not to notice either—for the third time that evening. Ellen had to give him credit. He might be a pompous money bag, like Mandy and Kimberly thought, but he was a *polite* pompous money bag.

"So," he wheezed, "which part of the Alps do you think your family's going to visit this Christmas?"

Ellen searched her mental map of the world. The Alps? How many parts were there? North Alps? South Alps? New Alps? Alpsville?

"Oh, goodness." Ellen shrugged, as if it made no difference to her. "Christmas is months away. Maybe we'll go to Mexico instead."

"Which part of Mexico?" Jared asked with interest.

Here we go again! Ellen decided it was a good thing she wasn't really rich. It would be pretty hard to go jetting around the world without the faintest idea where she was going.

Fortunately, Ellen didn't have to answer. They had reached the hotel, and Jared seemed to have something else on his mind. "Ellen," he began nervously. He pushed the button for the elevator.

"Yes?" she answered. Maybe he was going to break up with her, she thought happily. Maybe he was tired of getting jabbed in the ribs and talking to a girl who didn't know one Alp from another.

The elevator doors opened. Some girls stepped out, smiling at Ellen and Jared, and another couple appeared on the walkway and stepped into the elevator with them.

"I'll wait until we get upstairs," Jared said in a low tone, making it clear that whatever he had to say, it was private.

They rode the elevator up in silence. When the car arrived on the fourteenth floor, Jared said goodnight to the other couple and put a firm hand on Ellen's elbow.

Ellen guessed he wasn't taking any chances on getting jabbed again.

"Ellen," Jared began again as he walked her down the hallway toward her room, "I understand I'm not the only guy in your life. But I'd like to make sure I keep my place in the lineup."

Ellen paused with her hand on the doorknob. *Darn!* If he wasn't going to break up with her, maybe she should break up with him.

It was kinder, really. "Jared . . ."

Before she could say another word, she heard a burst of laughter from the room opposite. She could hear Kimberly's deep guffaw, Jessica's melodic laugh, Mandy's funny wheezing sound— and most important, Lila's high-pitched giggle!

Ellen drew in her breath. They were her best friends. Girls who had sacrificed their own fun and romantic dreams to make hers come true. She couldn't let them down. Couldn't let Lila down.

She gave Jared her warmest, most encouraging, and yet most aristocratic look. "Jared, you're a really special guy. You'll always have a place in the lineup."

Jared smiled happily, squeezed her hand, then ducked down the hall a few yards. He reached behind a large potted plant and removed a long, elaborately wrapped package. "I got this for you earlier today. I hid it before I picked you up so I could surprise you." He presented the gift to her.

Ellen stared at the package in astonishment. It was some package. The bow alone probably cost what Ellen usually spent on a dress.

Ellen unwrapped the gift and gasped. It was an expensive brand-named tennis racket.

Jared smiled at her. "I'm sure it's not as good as you're used to," he said in a humble voice. "But it was the best one they had."

Ellen tried to return his smile. Normally, she loved receiving presents. And she could picture herself running around the court at Sweet Valley Middle School with the racket. People would really think she was a hot player. But there was no way she could let Jared spend this kind of money on her.

She held the racket out to him. "I can't accept this."

"Why not?" Jared asked.

"It's way too—" Ellen broke off. How could she tell him that the raquet was too expensive? She was supposed to be one of the richest girls in the world.

A girl that rich wouldn't think a racket like the one he had given her was such an big deal.

She laughed—her rich eccentric laugh. "Well, I don't know." She waved the racket back and forth. "Oh I *do* know. It's not the right weight."

"Really?" Jared looked disappointed.

"You take it back," she said kindly. "It's the thought that counts, and I think you were really nice to want to give me something so special."

Jared smiled and leaned toward her. He pursed his lips, then hesitated. He gripped her elbow firmly, smiled, then pressed his lips against hers.

"That sounds like her laugh." Lila sat upright in the middle of the Unicorn meeting. She tiptoed toward the door, her friends at her heels.

Lila opened the door a crack and peered out. She could feel Mandy catch her breath behind her. Jared and Ellen stood in front of the door across the hall. Kissing!

Lila quietly shut the door. She didn't want to see any more.

"I'm making my move," Lila whispered to Mandy, Jessica, and Kimberly a few moments later. She had been listening through the closed door until Ellen and Jared said good night and parted ways. "Give me thirty seconds, and then you guys go to work."

Mandy, Jessica, and Kimberly nodded.

Lila took another look into the hall to make sure

Ellen was nowhere in sight, then she hurried out of the room, running quietly to catch up with Jared.

She stood behind him while he waited for the elevator, then slipped in behind him just as he was pushing the button for his own floor.

"Jared!" she said softly.

"Lila! What a surprise!" He looked around. "Where did you come from?"

"Jared," Lila said, "I have something to tell you. Something you need to know for your own good. It's about Ellen. . . ."

The doors closed, and Lila threaded her arm through Jared's. She was going to talk. And he was going to listen.

Mandy hurried along the covered outdoor walkway that led to the open-air lobby. She had called Jack and asked him to meet her in the corner of the lobby where the colorful birds gathered during the day.

Last night, the full moon had brightened the corner. Tonight, though, it was almost spooky. Dark clouds covered the moon, and wind whistled through the trees and the hallway.

She spotted Jack in the outdoor lobby area looking out toward the ocean. White ruffles rolled in toward the beach. His loose pants and white shirt billowed around him in the wind.

He looked so handsome and romantic, Mandy's knees began to wobble. "Hi," she said softly, hurrying over to stand beside him.

"Beautiful, huh?" he commented, his eyes fixed on some distant point.

"It is," Mandy agreed. "Wild and dark and beautiful." *Like you,* she added mentally.

He turned his brooding face toward hers. "You said you had something you wanted to talk to me about. Does it have anything to do with Ellen?"

"Let's walk along the water," she suggested. She stepped out of the lobby, and they wandered past the pool toward the beach in silence.

When they reached the sand, he took her hand and squeezed it. Mandy felt a little fluttering sensation around her shoulder blades. "Mandy," he began, "I think I know what you're going to tell me."

"You do?" she asked.

"Ellen probably asked you to talk to me, right? To tell me that she has a lot of guys and can't make any exclusive commitment." He smiled wistfully. "She doesn't want me to be hurt. Is that it?"

"Well, not exactly," Mandy told him, coming to a stop.

Jack gave her a quizzical look. "No?"

Mandy shook her head. "I wanted to tell you that you're all wrong about Ellen."

Jack put his hands on Mandy's shoulders. "You mean she *does* want an exclusive relationship?"

Mandy tried not to think about how hopeful and eager he looked. She took a deep breath. "No. I mean Ellen's not anything like you think she is. She's not artistic. She's not into crafts. She doesn't care about poetry or jewelery-making or anything like that."

Jack cocked his head and tucked his hair behind his ears. "Huh?"

"Ellen's a nice girl. But she's putting on an act to impress you," Mandy explained bluntly.

Jack pulled Mandy toward him and hugged her tightly. "Oh, Mandy," he said sadly. "How could I have been so blind?"

Mandy's heart thundered, and a million butterflies took flight in her stomach. She almost swooned. This was even better than she'd dreamed. She wrapped her arms around Jack's waist. Finally, he saw that Mandy was really the right girl for him.

"Poor Mandy," he said sadly.

Poor Mandy? She frowned. What did he mean, *"Poor Mandy?"*

He stroked her hair. "Poor, poor, Mandy. It must be so hard for you."

"Huh?" Mandy grunted into his chest.

"Ellen is everything you want to be, isn't she?" he whispered sadly. "I've noticed how you try to dress like her, and talk like her, and imitate her facial expressions."

Mandy felt the color drain from her face. "Ellen—I—she—"

Jack put his hands on her shoulders and held at arm's length. "Mandy, you can't build yourself up by tearing Ellen down. So don't try. Work at finding yourself. Finding your own style. Your own creative voice."

Mandy tried to speak, but she was so dumb-founded, all she could do was gurgle incoherently. Something that sounded vaguely like "Gllloo Bbbbb Gack!" escaped her throat.

"There you go," Jack said encouragingly. "Just keep at it and you'll learn to be Mandy Miller instead of a pale imitation of Ellen."

Jack backed away, disappearing in the reflected light from the beach. Mandy watched, her eyes filling with tears of frustration. "Gacckkk!" she choked.

"So, what you're basically saying is that Ellen doesn't like sports, doesn't like meditation, and doesn't like me?" Peter's blue eyes stared into Kimberly's.

They sat in the Café Misto drinking decaffeinated latte. Kimberly took a sip and set down her cup. "Well . . . it sounds weird, but yeah. See, I just told her to pretend to be interested in everything you said or did. So that's exactly what she did."

Peter bit his lower lip and thought hard for a moment. "Why?" he asked in a bewildered tone. "Why would you tell her to pretend to be interested in everything I said or did?"

"Because I wanted you to like her," Kimberly explained.

He looked at her quizzically. "Why? What's it to you whether I like Ellen or not?"

"I wanted Ellen to have a great guy," Kimberly blurted out. "And I thought you were a great guy. But I thought if you knew the *real* Ellen, you wouldn't like her. So I made her into somebody you would like."

Peter shook his head. "Let me see if I understand this. *You* thought I was a great guy. So you thought I would be perfect for *Ellen*—who, according to you, has nothing in common with me and no interest in anything that interests me. Kimberly, that makes absolutely no sense at all."

"It doesn't when you say it like that," Kimberly admitted, realizing how ridiculously far-fetched the whole story sounded now. "But I was just trying to be her friend."

Peter folded his arms. "So why are you telling me this? What are you trying to do?"

Kimberly took a deep breath. It was time to lay her cards on the table. Peter was a bright guy. He'd probably appreciate guts and honesty. "What I'm trying to do is tell you that Ellen is all wrong for you and I'm perfect. I'm the one who's into sports. I'm the one with a ton of energy. Ellen is a total couch potato. She lives on junk food. And if you want to know the whole truth, I've never considered her too bright."

Peter sat back in his chair. "I think I understand," he said slowly. He stared at her face as if he were seeing it for the first time. "I think I really get it."

Kimberly smiled. Finally! The thrill of victory made her pulse race.

Peter drained his cup of decaffeinated latte. "You're jealous of Ellen. So you're trying to sandbag her."

"Huh?" Kimberly's heart dropped. "I mean, no, that's not it at all!"

Peter put his cup down on the table with a thump. "Yeah! That's what it's all about. And it's not a pretty picture." He shook his head as if he were deeply disappointed. Then he stood. "You say you're her friend? Wow! With friends like you . . ." Peter didn't bother to finish. He just sort of sneered before turning away and walking toward the door.

"Peter!" Kimberly cried. "You've got it all wrong."

But Peter left the café without a backward glance.

"I am sooooo glad you called me," Sam said happily as he followed Jessica into the dessert court. "Talk about the perfect end to a perfect day! I went parasailing, had a swim with Ellen, ate a great big lobster dinner, and now I'm having dessert with a beautiful California girl who just happens to have my very favorite name—Jessica."

Sam gave the woman behind the counter a wide smile, and Jessica watched the magic power of Sam's enthusiasm. "Good evening," the lady said in a welcoming voice. "What would you like?"

"Jessica?" Sam prompted. "Something chocolate? Something with cream? Or something with both?"

"Something with both," Jessica said decisively. She pointed to a tall glass filled with chocolate cake, chunks of dark chocolate candy, strawberries, and whipped cream. "That!"

"Good choice. We'll take two." Sam paid for the desserts while Jessica collected napkins, spoons, and water and found them a table in a quiet corner.

She looked nervously around, hoping to find a table where they could talk privately. Luckily, the dessert court was about half full. Probably because it was late. Most people had probably gone to bed after a long day of water and beach activities. If she weren't so nervous, she'd be sleepy herself.

She scurried toward a quiet table for two in the corner and set a place for Sam and herself. Moments later, Sam placed her dessert in front of her. "For madam," he said solemnly.

Jessica laughed. "I'm glad you didn't go to bed early," she said. "Because I really need to talk to you."

Sam took a bite of his dessert and made an appreciative face. "MMMMMmmm. Now *that* is good. I'm so glad I had you along, because I might not have picked this dessert on my own."

Jessica took a bite. "It is good," she agreed. "But what I really needed to say was . . ."

Sam loaded his spoon with chocolate, cream, and a strawberry and shoved it in his mouth. "And what about this cream?" he said thickly. "Tastes like the real thing to me. Not canned. What do you think?"

Jessica took a tentative taste. "Yep. Authentic whipped cream. So, anyway . . ."

Sam took a big swallow of water, washing down the dessert, and smacked his lips. "And this water! Did you taste the water? Now, how can water taste this good?"

Jessica began to wish that Sam's unrelenting enthusiasm would let up for at least five minutes so she could talk.

"I'll bet their water comes from an underground spring," he said.

"Whatever," Jessica said, waving her spoon to try to get his attention. "But let's talk about Ellen for a minute."

"Ellen. Sure. My favorite subject. What's the most popular girl on the cruise doing tonight?"

Jessica stirred her dessert, mixing up the chocolate and the cream. "Well, this is exactly what I want to talk to you about. You see, I think you have a false impression of Ellen."

"A false impression?" Sam took another bite.

"Right. What I'm trying to say is that the girl you think Ellen is, she really isn't."

Sam laughed and swallowed. "Jessica, I'm just not following you at all. Are you and Ellen trying to play some kind of joke?"

"Look, Ellen isn't your type," Jessica said flatly, placing her spoon on the table. "And this isn't a joke. All that upbeat, enthusiastic stuff she does? It's an act. I mean, Ellen's a great friend of mine and everything, but just between you and me, she's kind of on the lazy side. Not to mention a space cadet. The Ellen Riteman who you think is so great doesn't exist. She's a figment of *my* imagination. I told her what to wear, what to say, and how to act—so she would attract guys. If you met the real Ellen, you wouldn't like her at all."

A little of the sparkle left Sam's eyes. He chewed thoughtfully and deliberately before swallowing. Then he pushed his dessert away.

Sam's mouth twisted, and Jessica couldn't tell if he was smiling or grimacing. He shifted nervously and scratched his head. "This is some kind of girl thing, right?" he asked uneasily. "You and Ellen are having an argument, and this is your way of settling the score?"

"I am *not* trying to settle a score," Jessica protested. She'd been prepared for him to argue with her about Ellen's true personality, but this accusation caught her off guard.

"Then why are you running Ellen down to one of her biggest fans?" he asked. "What's the point?"

Jessica breathed deeply, trying to stay calm and not sound defensive. "I'm trying to get you to see the truth. That Ellen isn't what you think, and that . . . and that . . ." Jessica broke off, embarrassed to say "I am."

Sam stared at her with big, hurt eyes. "And that what?"

Jessica knew it was now or never. "That *I* am the real upbeat and positive girl that Ellen pretends to be," she blurted out. "If you don't believe me, ask one of the other girls. Ask Kimberly. Or Lila. Or Mandy. They'll tell you."

Sam raised his eyebrows. "You don't sound too upbeat and positive right now."

Jessica blushed. He was getting the completely wrong idea about her. "You don't understand," she began to explain. "What I mean is—"

"I don't know what your problem with Ellen is,"

Sam broke in quietly, "but this isn't a good way to handle it. I don't like being used like this. I don't think you would either if you were me." He stood up and dropped his napkin on the table. "Good night, Jessica."

Jessica sat with her spine as stiff as a broomstick. Her cheeks felt hot, and her heart was beating like a drum. She'd made a complete fool out of herself. Sam didn't believe a word she'd said, and now he was probably more in love with Ellen than ever.

Ellen stood on the balcony and let the hard wind blow through her hair. It felt good, but the powerful gusts couldn't quite blow away the memory of all the ridiculous and stupid things she'd said that day.

She stepped back into the room, closed the sliding glass door of the balcony, and climbed into bed. She pulled the thick coverlet up to her chin with a groan.

Jack is a dark silhouette against the sun. Bright around the edges and an eternal mystery.

She couldn't believe that she could say stuff like that to a guy and that he would take it seriously.

She couldn't believe that she could elbow a guy in the ribs three times and he would act like he didn't notice.

She couldn't believe that any of her suitors actually fell for her act. In a strange way, it made her lose respect for them.

Ellen turned over and pulled the covers up over her head. Maybe there was something wrong with her, but she'd really rather spend time with her girlfriends. All that male attention was flattering, but she wasn't really interested in any of them. It was a chore spending time with people she didn't have anything in common with.

She wished the other Unicorns would find guys. Then they'd be busy with their own love lives and wouldn't have time to be so worried about hers. She could drop the poses and be herself—boring, whiny, uninteresting Ellen Riteman.

On the other hand, if her friends did find guys, they wouldn't be interested in hanging with Ellen. They'd all be right where they started on day one of the cruise. Mandy, Kimberly, Lila, and Jessica all guy-crazy. Ellen wandering around by herself.

She groaned again. Talk about a lose-lose situation.

The night-light in the bathroom created a warm glow. Ellen looked across the room at Lila's unmade bed. After Jared had brought her home, she'd given him about fifteen minutes to disappear. Then she had gone across the hall and knocked on the door. Nobody had answered, so Ellen had come back to her own room.

Ellen guessed they had all gone out somewhere together. She pictured them in one of the coffee bars or restaurants—laughing, talking, and having a great time without her.

A hot tear trickled down her cheek. The most popular girl on the *Dream Teen* cruise felt pretty left out right now.

She fiercely wiped the tears away and closed her eyes. As she fell asleep, her mind conjured up an image of a friendly sunburned face surrounded by white blond hair. It was too bad that the one guy who she *would* enjoy spending time with was on the forbidden list.

Curtis might be a phony.

But Ellen was a phony too.

They were perfect for each other.

But how would he ever know? She was surrounded by guys morning, noon, and night, and he was too laid back to fight for her. Unfortunately, Curtis Bowman just wasn't the competitive type.

Jared stared at Lila. His face was white, as if he were in shock. They were sitting in a deserted area of the lobby in wicker chairs only inches apart.

"I know it's hard to believe," Lila concluded. "But it's true. Ellen is nobody important at all. The Ritemans are just ordinary people from Sweet Valley. She's not rich. She's not aristocratic. She's just been pretending—so she could snag you. I thought it was time you finally heard the truth."

There was a long silence. Jared pressed his lips together and breathed through his nose, his nostrils flaring. It was clear to Lila that he was furious.

"Don't be angry at Ellen," she began, "it's—"

"Ellen!" he exploded. "I don't want to hear you say one word about Ellen!"

Lila shut her mouth with a snap and fought the impulse to grin like an idiot. This was fantastic. A dream come true. Jared sounded completely enraged! Like he *hated* Ellen. He'd probably never speak to her again. And that was fine with Lila.

Jared stood up. "Lila, I thought you were a nice girl. More than nice, actually. In fact, if it hadn't been for the way I felt about Ellen, I would have . . . "

Lila stood up and put her hand on Jared's arm. "It's not too late," she said quickly. "We can still get together."

He shook off her hand. "You and me!" Jared snorted, as if her suggestion was ridiculous. "Somebody like you could never be with somebody like me."

Lila's eyes opened wide. "What do you mean— *somebody like me?*"

"People like me, and like Ellen, we're targets for your type. Targets for opportunists who want to use us for our money and our position. Targets for spiteful people who are jealous of us because of what we have and who we are."

Lila gasped. "Are you accusing me of—"

"I'm telling you that you're the lowest of the low. Somebody who pretends to be a friend but who's really just a back-stabbing user."

"How dare you?" Lila demanded angrily. "I'm trying to help you."

"You're trying to break me and Ellen up," Jared accused.

"What's to break up?" Lila couldn't help retorting. "Do you have any idea how many guys Ellen is stringing along?"

"What's the matter, Lila? Jealous?"

A lump rose in Lila's throat. She was angry. She

was hurt. She was frustrated. And most of all, she was confused. How had this conversation gotten so out of control?

"You've probably been hanging on to Ellen's coattails for years," he sneered.

Lila began to shake. No one had ever spoken to her like this in her life. No one had ever accused her of such awful things. "Do you have any idea who I am?" she demanded between gritted teeth.

"No," he said angrily, his hands balled into fists. "But I know *what* you are. You're a snake."

With that, Jared stalked back to the elevators. He pushed the button and then turned. "Don't ever speak to me again!" he shouted before stepping into the elevator. Lila caught a last glimpse of his face before the elevator doors closed.

Sobs of anger, hurt, and bewilderment shook Lila's shoulders.

She'd been trying to put things right. To tell the truth. And the result was that he thought she was evil.

And it was all Ellen's fault.

Six

The next morning, Ellen tiptoed across the room. Lila slept heavily, and Ellen let herself out of the room as quietly as possible. She had been asleep when Lila came in last night, so she had no idea what time Lila had gone to bed.

Ellen figured that if Lila was that knocked out, the others were too. She decided to let them sleep.

She glanced at her watch. Maybe if she hurried down to breakfast early, she could dine without any of her princes hanging all over her for a change. She could use a little time to herself.

This morning, Ellen had actually put on one of her own outfits. Some jeans and a sweatshirt. She'd had enough of costumes.

She rode the elevator down. When the doors opened onto the outside lobby, she shivered. What had happened to the tropical paradise? The sky was a bleak color, and the air was chilly.

Captain Jackson came striding across the patio with another ship's officer. "Good morning, Ms. Riteman," he said.

"Good morning, Captain Jackson. What's with this weather?" she asked.

"The tropical storm moved in closer last night. I'd advise you not to wander off too far."

"No sir, I won't," Ellen answered nervously.

Captain Jackson made a gesture that looked like a cross between a salute and a wave and strode away with the other officer. The captain was a former navy officer, and it showed. He was totally intimidating. He reminded her of their school principal, Mr. Clark. Only Captain Jackson was a snappier dresser.

She hurried toward the breakfast buffet in the pool's pavilion. A selection of muffins had been arranged on a long table. Ellen took a large white plate with a gold border and loaded it up with five miniature muffins and some yogurt.

She sat down at a small table and prepared to enjoy a little solitary gluttony. It was nice to be off on her own. Nobody to impress. If she got blueberries stuck in her teeth, so what?

"Now that's what I call food!"

Ellen looked up and saw Curtis hovering a couple of feet away with a plate piled even higher than Ellen's. "Can I sit with you?"

"Sure," Ellen said eagerly. Curtis Bowman was

maybe the only person she could cope with this early. He sat down and pulled the metal tab off the top of his small juice can.

She watched his head bob on his shoulders as if he were listening to some kind of surfer music on invisible headphones. He smiled at her, and she smiled back.

She felt more relaxed than she'd been in a long time. Curtis didn't seem to expect her to make any conversation. He seemed perfectly content to eat muffins and listen to his imaginary music. There weren't too many people she could sit with in silence and not feel like she was being boring.

"Ellen!" Jack appeared next to her. Her heart sank slightly, but she curved her lips into a smile. She hoped he wouldn't expect another haiku. Haiku in the morning was probably more than her stomach could take.

Jack wore his customary black. A black sweatshirt over black shorts. Silver and abalone earrings dangled from his ears, and he wore slip-on black Keds. "Listen, I really need to talk to you." He shot a look at Curtis. "Privately," he added.

"Want me to sit someplace else?" Curtis asked good-naturedly.

"If you wouldn't mind," Jack said, barely looking at him.

Curtis picked up his plate. "Fun while it lasted," he said to Ellen, sidling off with his plate.

Ellen's appetite was suddenly gone. She turned

angrily toward Jack. "You know, that was really rude," she cried. "I thought you were so sensitive."

Jack sat down and leaned toward Ellen, lowering his voice so that no one sitting nearby could hear. "I'm sorry. But I really wanted to talk to you. Besides, I can't stand macho phonies. I'll bet that guy's never stood up on a surfboard in his life."

"Pretending to be something else isn't a crime," Ellen said quietly.

Jack looked struck for a moment. "I guess not." He fiddled with a dangling earring. He seemed to be thinking very hard. Ellen wondered if he was trying to think up an apology poem. A haiku.

Jack is a big fat jerk. Sensitive around the edges, but a critic to the core.

"There's something I think you should know," he said in a halting tone. "I wasn't going to tell you, but . . . I lay awake all last night and changed my mind. It's the kind of thing *I'd* want somebody to tell *me*."

"What is it?" Ellen asked. She couldn't imagine what Jack was going to tell her. Did she have spinach in her teeth or something? Did she spit when she talked? Did she smell bad?

"I'd rethink my friendship with Mandy if I were you," Jack suggested in a grave voice.

"Huh?" Ellen wasn't sure she'd heard him properly. Did he say she should rethink her friendship with Mandy?

"Mandy is not your friend," Jack continued in a melodramatic tone.

"Mandy is one of my very best friends," Ellen protested with a laugh. "What are you talking about?"

Jack's dark eyes burned with intensity. "She's not your friend. Trust me. When your back is turned, she says things about you that are . . . . well . . . " His voice cracked, and he broke off. He pushed a lock of hair off his brow and took some deep breaths. "Look, I don't want to get into it, but I thought you ought to know." He leaned forward and kissed her cheek. "I'll see you later." He left quickly, as if he were afraid he might cry.

Ellen stared across the dining room, feeling as if someone had just pulled her seat out from under her. Jack was very artistic and imaginative. Too imaginative. He must have overheard something Mandy said and misunderstood it. Now he was going way over the top. Did Mandy know about the misunderstanding? Ellen wondered.

She pushed her plate away and stood up. It was stupid to sit around wondering. She would ask Mandy herself.

"Ellen!" a deep voice called as she moved toward the door.

Ellen cringed. It was Peter. She turned and forced a smile. "Peter," she began, "I'm really glad to see you up so early but I just can't make it to yoga this morning—I've got some—"

"I need to tell you something," he said. His face was troubled, and a deep furrow creased his tanned brow.

He's breaking up with me, Ellen thought with

relief. What else could explain the pained and anguished look?

"It's about . . . one of your *friends*. And I use the term loosely."

"What?" Ellen knew her face had that stupid look on it that drove her friends crazy, but Peter didn't seem to notice.

Peter wiped his palms on the front of his shorts, as if he were very nervous. Then he cracked his knuckles as he spoke. "I don't like having to tell you this, but one of your friends is saying some pretty ugly things about you." He gave his second and third finger joints a loud snap for emphasis.

"Mandy?" Ellen asked.

"Mandy?" Peter repeated in a puzzled voice.

"What did Mandy say about me?" Ellen pressed. She was disappointed that Peter wasn't dropping her, but she hoped he might be able to shed a little light on the Mandy mystery. She was eager to get this misunderstanding cleared up as soon as possible.

Peter shifted on the balls of his feet and looked confused. "I don't know. I haven't talked with Mandy. I'm talking about Kimberly."

Ellen cleared her throat and wondered if she looked as dumb as she felt. None of this was making any sense at all. "*Kimberly* said bad things about me? When?"

"Last night," Peter said. "I'm not going repeat what she said. I don't even remember most of it. But she was making you out to be some kind of phony. I thought you ought to know. You seem to think she's a friend, but she's letting you down in a big way." He nervously tucked the hem of his tennis shirt into his shorts.

Ellen felt stunned and slightly sick. What *was* going on?

Peter put his arm around her and squeezed her shoulders. "Don't get all hung up on this, OK? Anger isn't healthy. And you don't need Kimberly for a friend. You can be your own best friend. Right?"

Ellen nodded and gently ducked out from beneath Peter's arm. "Right. But ummmm, listen . . . I need to go up to my room and . . . " She trailed off, too distracted to think up a plausible excuse.

"Can we get together later?" Peter called after her as she hurried across the patio toward the elevator.

Ellen didn't answer. She couldn't think fast enough. Something was wrong. Way wrong.

The wind was so strong now, some of the chairs beside the pool were rocking. She reached the elevator and jabbed the button with a mounting sense of panic.

Her hair whipped around her face, lashing her cheek. Finally, the little red light above the elevator dinged, and the door opened to reveal . . . Sam.

"Ellen! I've been looking for you." He reached forward and took her hand, pulling her into the elevator. He pressed the button for the first-floor lobby. "Let's take a walk. I need to talk to you."

The doors closed, shutting out the scream of the wind. Ellen was grateful for the sudden calm. She pushed fourteen. "I'd really like to," she choked, "but I need to talk to . . . " She broke off when the elevator doors opened onto the enclosed lobby and Sam pulled her out.

"You need to hear what I have to say." For once Sam wasn't smiling. He looked dead serious.

"What's wrong?" Ellen asked, beginning to tremble. These conversations were starting to sound awfully alike.

"Ellen, you're a great girl and you deserve a better friend than Jessica."

"What are you talking about?" Her voice sounded high and thin. Ellen swayed. This was unreal. It was a dream. Any minute she was going to wake up and . . .

"She's not your friend," he said angrily. Ellen had a hard time believing she was talking to Sam Sloane. Always-in-a-good-mood-never-a-bad-word-for-anybody Sam Sloane.

He put an arm around her shoulder to steady her. "I know it's hard to believe. If I hadn't heard her say the things she said with my own ears, I wouldn't believe it myself. Gosh, Ellen. I'm the most trusting guy in the world. And I realized last night, after I talked to Jessica, that you're as trusting as I am. And that meant I really owed it to you to tell the truth."

Ellen pulled away from Sam.

They were playing some kind of horrible joke on her. All the guys. They'd gotten together and decided to do this. Because they were mad at her. "I know what you're doing," she choked, her chest tightening.

"Ellen . . ." Sam said, holding out his hand.

"You and Jack and Peter are trying to teach me a lesson," she managed to say. "Right? Because I went out with too many guys. So you got together and . . ."

"Jack and Peter?" Sam repeated. "What do they have to do with this?"

"Stop pretending," Ellen screamed. "Let's all stop pretending. I'm sorry if I hurt your feelings. I'm sorry if I made you mad. I'm sorry for everything, but I think it's really disgusting that you guys would try to take away the one thing that's really important to me—my friends."

Ellen ran sobbing toward the elevator.

"Jessica is not your friend," Sam shouted out behind her. "Ellen! Please, wait. Please, listen."

Ellen pushed the elevator button over and over, but nothing happened. She decided to take the stairs. So what if it was fourteen stories?

She ran to the stairwell, yanked open the door, and screamed. Someone was standing there.

"Ellen! It's me." Jared held out his arms, and she fell into them, sobbing. Jared was so strong and protective. He couldn't be part of this practical joke. He would never participate in anything like that. It would be beneath him.

"Oh, Jared," she sobbed gratefully. "I'm so glad you're here. I need somebody to be on my side."

"It's Lila, isn't it?" Jared asked angrily. "What did she say to you?" Jared's arms tightened around her shoulders.

Ellen's hands suddenly went cold. She broke out

of Jared's embrace and began backing away. "What about Lila?" she choked.

"I told her she was a back-stabber and a pathetic phony," Jared said, holding his hands out to Ellen. "I told her she wouldn't get away with . . ."

Ellen didn't let him finish. "No. No. No. I can't stand any more of this. I don't believe any of you. Jessica is my friend. So is Kimberly. And so is Mandy. Stop saying those horrible things."

"They may be your friends," Jared agreed. "But Lila Fowler is not. She's out to get you. She's trying to hurt you."

"She's not," Ellen argued. "I don't believe you. You're playing some horrible joke."

Jared plunged his hand into the paper bag he was carrying. "Look!" he insisted. He pulled out one of the red shoes Ellen had worn to dinner the night she had pretended to faint in Captain Jackson's private dining room in order to cover up a klutzy fall.

Now she really did feel faint. Her head was spinning. She couldn't seem to put it all together.

Jared took her arm and led her to a little upholstered bench. "Captain Jackson asked me to see that you got these back," he said gravely. "I put them in my room and forgot them. But after I talked to Lila, I started thinking. Wondering. And . . . look. You can see for yourself."

Jared handed Ellen one of the high-heeled shoes. The heel was broken off. "Lila lent me these shoes. I guess this one broke off when I fell . . . fainted," Ellen said.

"It didn't *break*," Jared said grimly. "The heel was

sawed almost halfway through." He reached into the bag and pulled out the other shoe. "They were both sawed through. Lila was probably hoping you would fall. I guess to embarrass you and make you look foolish."

"But I didn't really faint," Ellen murmured. "I fell. I tripped and . . ."

"You didn't trip. You fell because your heels collapsed. And they collapsed because Lila weakened them," Jared insisted.

Ellen examined the heels. They did look as if they had been sawed through. Would Lila really do something like that? And had the other girls known? She dropped the shoe and walked blindly toward the door to the stairwell.

"Where are you going?" Jared asked.

Ellen broke into a run, grabbed the stairwell door, and yanked it open.

"Ellen!" Jared called out.

But Ellen didn't answer. She had to talk to her friends. They *were* her friends, no matter what the guys said. It was all some kind of misunderstanding. It had to be.

"I hate it when she pretends to know a lot about nutrition," Kimberly Haver said bitterly. "I think that of all the things I hate about Ellen, I hate that the most. She's so incredibly pretentious. I don't know why Peter won't face the truth about her. She's obviously an idiot."

"Peter is an idiot," Jessica snapped. "Almost as big an idiot as Ellen." Jessica decided she was glad that Kimberly was a totally irritating grumpy crank of a person—it made her feel OK about biting her head off. And if felt really good to lash out at *some*body.

"Peter makes straight A's," Kimberly snarled. "What's Mr. GeeHowWonderful's grade point average?"

"Who cares?" Jessica couldn't help shrieking. "All I know is that he's a fabulous guy and he hates me and loves Ellen Riteman, who's nothing but this big bump on a log that we, because we're nice people, let be our friend. But when she sees Sam, she's Ms. Perky. Happy. Happy. Happy."

"She is such a phony," Lila said bitterly.

"Completely imitative," Mandy agreed.

"We've got to figure out how to get Ellen out of our lives and . . ." Jessica broke off when the door across the hall slammed. She looked at her friends with alarm.

"Was that the door to *my* room?" Lila whispered.

Mandy hurried to the door. "Oh, no. This door was open a crack. If that was Ellen going into the room across the hall, then she must have heard us talking."

"I'm sure it was a door down the hall," Kimberly insisted.

Mandy put her hands to her face, distressed. "Guys. What if it *was* Ellen?"

Jessica tossed her hair behind her shoulders. "If that was Ellen, then she shouldn't have been eavesdropping. Whatever she heard serves her right." She knew she wasn't being very nice, but she just didn't care. Her feelings were hurt—why shouldn't Ellen's be hurt too?

Kimberly folded her arms and flexed her knee. "Jessica's right. Personally, I don't care if Ellen heard. The truth never hurt anybody—except us."

Mandy walked around the room, her hands nervously twisting the hem of her leopard-print blouse. "Guys! We were saying some pretty awful things. Ellen's sensitive and . . ."

"Give it a rest, Mandy." Lila reached for Jessica's hairbrush and ran it through her hair. "You don't have to worry about everybody's feelings all the time."

Mandy's cheeks were flushed. "You know, it wouldn't kill any of you to worry about someone else's feelings once in a while." She looked at Lila. "Give me the key to your room, Lila. I want to go check and see if that was Ellen."

"Whatever." Lila rolled her eyes and handed Mandy the key.

"Well, is anyone coming with me?" Mandy wanted to know.

Kimberly harumphed.

Lila stretched out on the bed as though she hadn't even heard.

Jessica felt the slightest flicker of guilt. She had to admit, she and her friends had said some pretty harsh things. If Ellen had heard, she'd be really bummed out.

Then again, Ellen had basically stolen Jessica's dream man. Did someone like that deserve an apology? Jessica let her face fall into the most disinterested expression she could muster and turned away from Mandy, reaching for the other hairbrush on the dresser.

"Well, fine." Mandy left the room in a hurry. Jessica heard her working the key in the lock across the hall. There was a creak, and then Mandy cried out, "Oh, no! Guys! Come here. Quick!"

Jessica felt a pang of alarm—Mandy sounded panicked. Jessica dropped the brush and raced from the room with Lila and Kimberly behind her.

"Oh, wow!" Jessica breathed, practically falling into Lila and Ellen's room.

The room looked like a tornado had blown through. Ellen's dresser drawers had been emptied and tossed on the floor. A few empty hangers in the closet swung back and forth as if garments had been snatched off them a few seconds before.

Lila looked under the bed. "Her suitcase is gone," she announced.

Guilt welled up in Jessica's throat, but she choked it back down. She was sick of Ellen Riteman dominating her entire vacation. "Good riddance," she said defiantly.

Seven

"Excuse me," Ellen said for the fifth time. There seemed to be twenty phones ringing at once, and the harried concierge galloped from one end of the counter to the other, answering the phones and gibbering in French. He seemed upset, but Ellen didn't see why he couldn't acknowledge her. She was pretty upset herself.

A little silver desk bell stood at her left elbow. Ellen pounded on it with her palm.

Ding. Ding. Ding. Ding.

The concierge dove toward her and almost threw himself over the bell. "Mademoiselle?" he asked irritably.

"I want to leave," Ellen said tearfully. "I need a taxi to take me to the nearest airport."

The concierge rolled his eyes. "Please,

mademoiselle. Don't be foolish. And do not be overly alarmed. Tropical storms are a fact of Caribbean life, and as long as you stay indoors and follow instructions, you have nothing to fear."

"I'm not afraid of the storm," Ellen retorted. "I just want to leave the island and go home. Is there an airport or something?"

"There is a small airstrip on the other side of the island. But the planes are grounded."

"Thank you," Ellen said. She hoisted her suitcase and headed for the ground-level lobby. At least if there was an airport, she could wait there until the storm was over and then get on the first flight going anywhere where there were no Unicorns.

Ellen reflected on what the concierge had said. The other side of the island, huh? Well, that sounded simple enough. If Ellen cut across the pool area, headed away from the shoreline, and kept going straight, she would reach the other side of the island eventually. She had to. It was some kind of science principal.

Outside, the wind was blowing hard, and the sky was growing darker by the minute. Hotel staff were busily moving furniture into a large shed off the pool area. The palm trees swayed. The fronds rustled ominously.

The party is over, and I am outta here, Ellen thought, clutching the handle of her suitcase.

"What's going on?" Lila said as the girls stepped off the elevator into the second-floor lobby.

Mandy had calmed down a little about the Ellen situation, figuring that she had just gone back to the boat. They'd catch up with her eventually.

But the chaos in the lobby was making her a little nervous. People were running in all different directions, shouting in French and English. Phones rang nonstop.

"It probably has to do with the storm," Kimberly commented. "There's Captain Jackson! Let's ask him."

Mandy felt her alarm recede a little. Captain Jackson looked so calm and relaxed. He couldn't look that way if anything too terrible was happening. "Captain Jackson! What's all the excitement about?"

He turned a grave face toward Mandy. "The storm is moving in fast. Faster than we expected. And it looks like it may hit hard."

"Are we talking typhoon?" Jessica squeaked.

"I do not encourage you to overdramatize the situation," Captain Jackson said in a frosty tone. "But I also want to make sure you understand the potential dangers. Mr. DeVille, the manager of the hotel, will be making an announcement in a moment. And hotel staff are going from room to room to alert the guests to the dangers. From now on, please do not attempt to use the elevators. And please don't leave the grounds."

Mandy pictured the empty room upstairs. The swinging hangers. The empty drawers. "Captain Jackson, I think one of our friends may have left to go back to the boat," she said.

Captain Jackson shook his head. "That would be impossible. We're getting ready to move the ship out several miles to avoid damage to the dock. The crew has instructions not to take on any passengers. So from here on, authority over the members of the Dream Teen Cruise will be in the hands of the island Coastal Patrol and Mr. DeVille."

"But . . . ," Mandy began.

He smiled. "Be good girls and do as you're told and everything will be fine. I'll see you after the storm," he said, disappearing into the crowd.

Mandy watched him leave with a growing sense of unease. Ellen had taken her suitcase. But she couldn't have gotten far. Surely she would have turned around and come back when the weather turned this bad.

"I'm sure Ellen's around here somewhere," Jessica muttered. "I mean, she has to be. Right?"

"She'll turn up," Kimberly said with a noticeable lack of enthusiasm. "She always does."

"Like a bad penny," Lila agreed.

Mandy watched two hotel clerks stretch masking tape across the plate glass windows and hoped the other girls were right.

Ellen squinted. The rain was coming down so hard, she couldn't see more than three feet ahead. She couldn't figure out which way she was going.

She'd envisioned simply walking across the island in a straight line. That was turning out to be harder than she had anticipated.

St. Maurice was a volcanic island, elevated at the center and covered with thick jungle. Ellen wasn't sure where she was in relation to the neatly manicured grounds of the hotel. She kept getting turned around.

She looked out toward the ocean, trying to get her bearings.

The waves were huge. Rising higher and higher before collapsing against the rock outcroppings.

Ellen's toe snagged a root. She fell forward with a cry. The next thing she knew, she was facedown on the wet ground. Rain pounded her back like a thousand tiny fists.

She slowly got up on her hands and knees, then tried to stand. A terrible pain shot through her ankle. She cried out again and fell against a tree.

Very carefully, she turned her foot around on her ankle. It wasn't broken. But the area around the bone throbbed with a dull ache. Which probably meant she wouldn't make it to the other side of the island.

I'll go to the ship, she thought. She could take refuge there. Somebody could drive her to the airport when the storm was over.

"Attention. Attention, please." The hotel manager walked through the packed second-floor lobby speaking through a bullhorn. "Please be quiet, boys and girls. I need your attention."

The lobby was packed with guys and girls talking, laughing, and frightening each other with stories about storms and hurricanes. The noise was deafening.

Mandy and the other Unicorns drew closer to hear what the hotel manager had to say. The double doors to the large dining room were open, and Mandy watched the rain beat against the glass.

She was really worried now. Ellen had never appeared in the lobby. Every half an hour, they had taken turns going up the thirteen flights of stairs to see if Ellen had by some chance managed to slip past them and gone back to the room.

It had now been two hours since Captain Jackson had left, and Mandy was convinced that Ellen was not in the hotel.

The hotel manager had a pencil-thin mustache, light brown skin, and a slight French accent. He wore black pants and a white shirt with a little plastic name tag over the pocket that said Mr. DeVille. He'd been around the hotel grounds non-stop for the last three hours.

"May I have your attention?" he asked again through his bullhorn.

Slowly, the loud chatter began to die away.

Then the manager climbed up on a coffee table and addressed the group. "I am Mr. DeVille, the hotel manager. As you are no doubt aware, a severe storm is in progress. I have just been informed that weather officials have upgraded the storm to hurricane status."

Mandy's heart froze in her chest.

"It is imperative that you do not leave the hotel," the manager continued. "I repeat. It is imperative that you do not leave the hotel and that you follow any and all instructions given by the hotel staff. This is for your own safety. Thank you for your co-operation and we will keep you informed."

"Ellen's out there," Mandy whispered hoarsely.

Kimberly's face turned pale. "On foot," she added.

Jessica's eyes were large with worry. "We've got to do something or . . ." Her lip trembled. A tear rolled out of her eye and down her cheek. "It's my fault," she whispered.

Lila pressed her hands against her cheeks as if she were about to faint. "No it's not," she said. "It's mine. I did horrible things to Ellen. Sawing those heels. Setting her up to look dumb. What was I thinking?"

"You weren't thinking, and neither was I." Kimberly shoved her hands down into the pockets of her sweater and turned a miserable face toward Mandy. "None of us were, except Mandy."

Mandy was so scared, her fingertips felt numb. If anything happened to Ellen, it was her fault as much as anybody else's. She would never stop blaming herself. Never. She had to do something.

Mandy pushed her way through the crowd till she reached the hotel manager. "Mr. DeVille," she cried.

"*Oui?*" Mr. DeVille stopped and lifted his brows politely, but Mandy could *feel* his impatience.

"A friend of ours is missing," she said urgently. "We think she left on foot about three hours ago."

Mr. DeVille waved his hand. "Nonsense. Where would she go in this kind of weather?"

"That's the twenty-four-thousand-dollar question,"

Kimberly said, appearing at Mandy's shoulder along with Lila and Jessica. "We don't know. We were hoping you might have some ideas about where to look."

Mr. DeVille sighed. "Girls. If your friend did, indeed, leave the hotel, then she would have returned immediately when she realized that weather conditions were worsening." He sounded as if he resented being detained for such a trivial matter.

Mandy chewed her lower lip. What Mr. DeVille said was so logical. And he sounded so confident. But then, if he was right, where was Ellen? She felt like saying it out loud, but she was afraid he might get angry.

Mandy turned toward Jessica and opened her eyes wide—sending her the universally recognized "do something" signal. She knew she could count on Jessica for one thing: She never gave up. She was persistent to the point of being a pest when she wanted something.

Jessica stepped forward and looked Mr. DeVille in the eye. "You don't understand. Our friend was very upset. She's a little spacey on her best days, but when she's upset, she really doesn't think clearly. At *all*. I mean, we could tell you stories . . ."

Kimberly broke in. "And she loses her way like that." She snapped her fingers for emphasis.

Lila stepped closer. "Here's the bottom line. Our friend is out in the storm. And *we* want *you* to call the coast guard. Or whatever."

"Mr. DeVille!" Two hotel workers on the other

side of the lobby were trying to get Mr. DeVille's attention. They had a big cart piled high with blankets and water bottles. "Shall we distribute these now?" the taller of the two men asked.

"I'll be right there," Mr. DeVille told them. He edged out of the tight circle the girls had formed around him. "The island Coastal Patrol is very busy securing small craft and evacuating residents. I know that teenage girls love drama and excitement, but please don't get carried away. I'm sure if you look around, you will find your friend." He smiled indulgently. "The staff has put out sandwiches and cookies in the main dining room. Why don't you go in, have something to eat, and try not to worry." He patted Mandy's shoulder and hurried away, snapping his fingers to attract the attention of an assistant. "Jacques. How many blankets were you able to locate?"

"He doesn't believe us," Mandy said in a small voice.

"Maybe he's right," Kimberly said. "No matter how upset Ellen was, she would come back when the weather got this bad. She'd *have* to."

"If she *could*," Jessica added.

"Come on," Mandy said. "Let's go look around the dining room. Maybe we did miss her somehow."

Mandy led the girls through the crowd into the dining room. "Excuse me, excuse me," she murmured. The crowd parted, and Mandy let out a little scream.

Staring right at her were four pairs of the most accusatory eyes she had ever seen.

Jack, Peter, Jared, and Sam sat at a table with sodas and glared malevolently at the Unicorns.

"Well, well, well, look who's here. All of Ellen's very best friends," Jack drawled. "Where is Ellen, by the way?"

Mandy felt her heart sink. Jack was really going to hate her now. But not any more than she hated herself.

The wind screamed in Ellen's ears as she limped along. She'd never heard anything like it in her whole life. She stopped to rest her ankle and get her bearings. The rain pounded her face, and her hair whipped around her eyes. She raked it away and squinted. She was going the wrong way—again! The ocean had been to her right before, but now she could see it to her left.

A sound like a freight train came screaming past the trees. It was so savage and frightening that Ellen screamed herself. Suddenly, a gust of wind hammered her body and knocked the suitcase from her hand.

Ellen dove toward a tree trunk and wrapped her arms around it. The wind pushed against her, and she hid her face, pressing her cheek against the hard, rough bark for protection. As abrasive as it was, the wind was worse.

Her feet began slowly slipping out behind her. She clutched at the tree trunk and held on for dear life. "I've got to get to the ship," she sobbed. "I've got to get to the ship."

She lifted her head and shook her hair away like

a dog. She squinted through the punishing rain and wind for a glimpse of the ocean.

Finally, she saw it. And her heart sank down into her wet and soggy shoes.

The *Caribbean Queen* was putting out to sea, moving away from the island. "I give up," she cried, her lips trembling.

She would have to go back to the hotel. But where was it?

She looked around. Suddenly, she realized just how lost she was. She didn't have the faintest idea which way the hotel was. Ellen turned her head toward the ocean again. Miles offshore, the ship rocked and tossed in the ferocious sea.

A wave began rolling in, getting taller and taller. Ellen held her breath. She had never seen anything like it in her life. It broke near the beach, but Ellen couldn't help wondering how long it would be until the waves moved inland and washed her away.

"You mean Ellen is out there in that storm!" Jared thundered.

Lila had never seen anybody look so angry in her life—unless you counted Jack, Peter, and Sam.

Mandy nodded. "I know you think we're horrible. We think we're pretty horrible too. And we're sorry about everything." She reached for her rain slicker.

So did Jessica and Kimberly.

"Where are you guys going?" Sam asked.

Mandy shrugged. "To look for Ellen," she answered.

Peter shook his head. "But Mr. DeVille said . . ."

Jessica secured her blond hair into a ponytail. "We know you guys think we're creeps and bad friends. But we're a club. That means we hang tight. No matter what."

"You're going out there to look for her?" Jack asked.

Mandy nodded. "You bet."

Jack stood. "I'll go with you." He grabbed the jacket folded over the back of his chair.

"Me too," Peter said, standing up.

"We'll work in pairs," Jared suggested. "Split up and fan out in four directions."

"We're going to have to move fast," Sam said.

Mandy buttoned her red slicker. She could feel Jack's eyes on her. But she couldn't meet them. She was too ashamed.

Ellen clutched the tree trunk for dear life. Overhead, she heard an awful squeaking and tearing. It was either the biggest squirrel in the world, or else the wind was tearing branches off the tree. She looked up, but leaves, rocks, and gravel showered toward her face, and she lowered her head.

It was useless to scream for help. Who could hear her over this hellacious noise?

Sheets of rain blew in every direction, slapping her face and her back, and pounding on the side of her head.

Ellen crouched as low as she could, trying desperately to remember what she had been told to do in case of storms. *Stay away from trees.* Oh, great. She was surrounded by trees. And right now, this tree was the only friend she had. If she let go, she'd blow right out toward the beach and probably into the ocean.

Suddenly, something grabbed her and pulled, determined to break her hold on the tree trunk.

Ellen screamed and struggled as much as she could with both arms wrapped around a tree.

A strong arm wrapped around her waist, and a hand squeezed the muscle just above Ellen's elbow—hitting the nerve. Ellen let out a shriek and reflexively released her hold on the tree.

Immediately, she and her attacker went tumbling across the jungle floor, rolling over and over in the leaves and mud. "Let me go," Ellen shrieked. *"Let me go!"*

Eight

"Where are you going?" A hotel security guard stepped right in Jessica's path as she and the Unicorns and the guys headed for the stairwell.

The guard wore a brown rain slicker with fluorescent orange trim. His hat was covered in plastic, and he carried a walkie-talkie. Jessica saw three more security guards enter from the Employees Only door and begin stationing themselves around the large lobby area.

"We want to get a look at the storm up close," Jessica lied. The guard shook his head. "Sorry. No one is allowed to leave now. It is too dangerous. Please return to the dining room."

Jessica heard Jared whistle, Jack groan, and Sam make an impatient noise.

The walkie-talkie sprang to life with a rattle of

static, and the guard lifted it to his lips and began speaking rapidly in French.

Jessica motioned to the others to follow her a few feet away and gather around.

"Now what?" Jared said.

"We need someone to create a diversion," Jessica whispered. Her eyes flickered around the room, searching for an accomplice. She spotted Anna and Tommy Beardsley, playing cards with Danny Orisman and Kickie Crookshank.

Ellen's chin bounced off roots and rocks as two strong hands dragged her across the floor of the jungle. Her hands scrabbled wildly along the ground, trying to grab on to a bush or a branch.

The hands let go of her jeans, but before she could get her bearings, a pair of strong arms hooked her under the shoulders and pulled her to her feet. Ellen threw wild, blind punches, but the arms tightened like a vise and pulled her along.

Suddenly, miraculously, the wind and rain stopped. Her attacker released his hold, and Ellen stumbled and fell.

"Oh, man! Sorry."

Ellen raked the hair from her face and opened her eyes, blinking away dirt, water, tears, and windburn. "Curtis!" she cried.

She was in a cave . . . with Curtis Bowman! If she didn't hurt in about fifty-seven places, she'd think she was dreaming.

Curtis stood there, wearing a blue full-body wet suit. He squatted down next to her and brushed some of the dirt from her face. "Man! I was trying to tell you it was me, but I guess you couldn't hear me over the wind. What are you doing out here?"

"What am *I* doing out here?" she sputtered. "What are *you* doing out here?"

He grinned. "I *was* surfing. But the waves got too big—even for me."

"We're all going to die!" Anna Beardsley shrieked at the top of her voice. "We're going to die, I tell you." She jumped out of her chair, ran to the center of the room, and wailed, "I'm too young to die!"

A roar went up as Anna's panic spread through the dining room.

"I think my directing debut is a success," Danny Orison whispered to Mandy. "I can't wait to tell my dad. Of course I couldn't have done it without help from Anna. Wow! What an actress!"

Mandy giggled and prepared herself for Jessica's cue to move.

Anna Beardsley clutched her brow, rolled her eyes upward, and swooned.

Tommy ran to her side. "Help! Help! My sister is having some kind of attack!"

While the security guards and all the other adults on the premises rushed into the dining room to see about Anna, Mandy and the others moved backward into the lobby.

Jessica stood by the exit to the stairwell. She flashed an upturned thumb at Mandy and disappeared through the door. Behind her, Lila, Jared, Kimberly, Peter, Jack, Jessica, and Sam slipped out.

Mandy cast a last look around to be sure no one was watching. Mr. DeVille, the security guards, and the hotel staff were tending to Anna and trying to quiet the panic.

Mandy slipped into the stairwell and closed the door.

Jack was waiting for her. "This way," he whispered. He led her down the cement stairs. The electricity was out, and the small emergency light cast a dim, sickly yellow beam in the windowless concrete stairwell.

It was dank inside the stairwell, and Mandy shivered. "Wow! It's actually *cold* in here."

"The temperature's dropping," Jack explained. "Let's hope we find Ellen before it gets colder."

The ten-pound weight in Mandy's stomach began to feel more like twenty.

"So . . . you really *are* a surfer?" Ellen said incredulously.

Curtis grinned. "Sure. North American champion in my age range two years in a row."

"But why are you surfing in this weather?"

Curtis pushed his wet hair back off his forehead. "The best waves are right before a hurricane. I mean, they are *awesome*. It's not a smart thing to do, but as soon as I saw those tubes, I grabbed the board I rented and headed for the beach. I had some wild rides, man." His eyelids lowered as if he were remembering some sublime sensation. Then he gave her a rueful grin. "But I got knocked off, and the board broke up on some rocks. I'll have to pay for it. There goes the old Christmas money. But it was worth it."

Ellen began to laugh. The more she thought about it, the funnier it got.

"What's so funny?" Curtis asked.

"Everybody thought you were a phony."

"A phony what? And who's everybody?"

"My friends thought you were a phony surfer," Ellen explained. "They thought you were somebody pretending to be somebody else."

"Why would they think that?" Curtis asked.

Ellen blushed. "Because most of us are pretending to be something we're not. At least one of us." She drew in her breath. "Curtis, I'm not what you think I am. I'm not popular with guys. Not really. And I'm not smart or artistic or rich or anything special at all."

"I think you're a great girl," he said, meeting her gaze squarely. "And that's kind of hard to fake." He leaned forward, and Ellen's heart skipped a beat. But before his lips met hers, he reared back and cupped his ear. "Wait a minute. Listen."

Ellen's eyes searched the dark cave. "I don't hear anything."

Curtis's eyes cut toward the mouth of the cave. "I know. The wind died."

They moved toward the cave entrance and cautiously stepped out.

Ellen's tight shoulders relaxed. There was no rain and wind. It was quiet. "It's over!" She laughed and threw her arms in the air. "We're safe."

Curtis tugged at his earlobe, looking anxious. "Uhhhh, not really."

"What?"

"This is the eye," he explained. "A hurricane is like a big circle of weather. One side's passed over, and the other side's on the way."

Ellen's shoulders bunched again. She began to shiver in her wet jeans and sweatshirt. "You mean?"

Curtis looked up at the sky, his face grim. "Yeah. The worst is yet to come."

Ellen felt like somebody whose winning lottery ticket had just been invalidated. "Bummer," she muttered.

Mandy picked her way carefully across the wet ground. Broken branches were everywhere. If there was a path, it was impossible to discern. And if Ellen had left any kind of tracks or footprints, it would be impossible to find them now.

She shivered inside her slicker.

"Cold?" Jack asked.

Mandy nodded.

"Here," he said. "Take my jacket."

"But . . ."

"It's not raining," he said curtly. "I don't need it, and it'll keep you warm." He draped it around Mandy's shoulders, and Mandy immediately felt warmer.

Jack smiled faintly. "That better?"

"Yes," she said softly, wishing with all her heart that things between them could be different. Her eye rested on something hanging from a limb, and she gasped and dove for it. She snatched it from the tree.

"What is it?" Jack asked.

"It's Ellen's," Mandy answered. She held the shawl she had made Ellen. It was a lightweight wool. Mandy had embroidered little Unicorns around the border. The shawl was dirty now. And wet.

Jack turned the shawl over in his hands. "OK. Well, we know she came this way." He ran his fingers over the embroidery. "This is nice work. Who made this?"

"I did," Mandy answered softly.

Jack raised one eyebrow and turned the shawl over. In the corner, Mandy had embroidered, "To Ellen. With Love From Mandy."

"You did make this," Jack said in quiet surprise. "It must have taken a lot of time."

Mandy nodded. "It did. But I wanted to give Ellen something nice. Her parents were getting a divorce, and she was going through a really bad time. I wanted her to know that . . ." A lump rose in Mandy's throat.

"Wanted her to know what?" Jack asked quietly.

"I wanted her to know that I cared," Mandy choked. Tears began streaming down her cheeks. She felt horrible. Ellen hadn't wanted to pose and posture for the guys. Her friends had talked her into it. Ellen had done exactly what they had pressured her to do, and then they had all turned on her.

Jack put his arm around Mandy and pulled her closer to him. "Come on," he said softly. "Let's see if we can find some sort of trail."

Kimberly dug the heels of her lug-soled boots into the mud. She and Peter were on an upward sloping path, and Kimberly could feel the muscles in her legs working hard.

Some pretty violent weather had passed over this portion of the island, and there would be more coming after the eye. But at least she was moving. The exercise was keeping her calm. "I don't think Ellen would have come this way," she said.

"What makes you think that?" Peter asked, frowning.

"It's uphill and slippery. Ellen is strong. But if the wind were blowing, she couldn't have made it even this far up."

Peter nodded. "You're right. So what do you suggest?"

Kimberly looked around and spotted a long, flat area several yards below them. She pointed.

"She might have taken that route. Come on, let's check it out."

She hurried down the slope, angling her feet to keep her balance in the mud.

"You handle yourself very well," Peter commented, watching her agile descent.

It was the first thing Peter had said to her that wasn't strictly business. The first thing that wasn't along the lines of "You go this way, and I'll go that way."

"This is easy," Kimberly said with a grateful laugh. "It would be fun if I weren't so worried about Ellen." She hopped up on a fallen log and crossed a big mud puddle, using her arms for balance. Peter followed. "You handle yourself well too," Kimberly added.

Peter didn't answer for a long moment. He kicked some mud off his boot and turned the collar of his windbreaker up. "I . . . ummm . . . I came down pretty hard on you. I mean, I can tell you and the other girls really do care about Ellen. So why the slam?"

Kimberly reddened. "Because we were just stupid," she said. "We all tried to turn Ellen into copies of ourselves so she could attract what we each thought was the perfect guy. When it worked, we got jealous."

Peter puffed his cheeks and blew out his breath, as if the whole concept was just too complicated for him. "I think I need to think about that."

"Take your time," Kimberly answered. She moved on, pushing wet branches and vines out of her way.

She'd said what she had to say. Peter would either

forgive her or he wouldn't. Her biggest concern now was finding Ellen.

She reached the edge of a murky swamp about ten feet wide. Too wide to jump. Kimberly knelt down and inspected the water, trying to gauge the depth. "I can't tell if this is just a shallow spillway, or a pond."

Peter knelt down beside her. "Either way, she wouldn't have tried to cross this with a suitcase, would she?"

"It might not have been this wide or this deep before the storm," Kimberly pointed out. "It might have been a narrow trickle and it could have been clear before the rain and the debris hit it."

"You're right." Peter pulled off a boot. "I'll wade in and see what I can find out."

"That's too dangerous." Kimberly grabbed his arm. "It could be deep. Or the bottom could be full of suction holes."

"I don't see what choice we have," Peter said. "If Ellen crossed it, then she's on the other side and she's stranded."

"Wait a sec." Kimberly spotted a battered rowboat wedged between two trees several yards away. "I've got an idea. Give me a hand with that boat."

"That boat will never float," Peter said impatiently. "Half the hull is missing."

"I don't want it to float. Come on. Help me." Kimberly grabbed the side of the boat and jiggled it until it loosened.

Peter went around the trees and shoved it hard from the other side.

The rowboat came loose and, miraculously, it held together.

"OK!" Kimberly said. "You take the back, I'll take the front."

Together, they carried the old rowboat back to the swamp and set it down in the water. Kimberly pushed it until it bridged the water.

The rowboat swayed for a moment before it started taking in water. Ten seconds later, it made a glub glub sound and began to sink below the surface.

When the waterline reached the three-quarter mark on the hull, the boat settled.

"Good thinking," Peter said, grinning. "It's sitting on the bottom. So we just walk across. Right?"

"After you," Kimberly said, holding out her arm.

Peter stepped across the rowboat bridge, using the seats as stepping stones. "You know, Kimberly?" he said with a smile as she crossed the bridge to join him. "I'm beginning to like the way you operate."

Nine

"We're running out of time," Jessica said, carefully climbing the rocky pile of boulders that looked out over the beach. "We'd better—"

"Get away from the water before the second part of the storm blows in," Sam finished. It was the tenth time he had finished her sentence for her. He grimaced. "Sorry. That can be an irritating habit."

"I don't think it's irritating," Jessica said. "It just tells me we're thinking like a team."

He laughed mirthlessly. "That's an upbeat spin."

Jessica took a deep breath. Sam was determined to keep her at arm's length. He wasn't unfriendly or hostile. But he wasn't his warm, accepting self either.

Sam reached out and took her hand, helping her off the boulders. "See if you can guess what I'm thinking now."

"You're thinking that we've covered about a mile of ground and haven't seen anything between here and the hotel," Jessica guessed. "That we've circled the perimeter of the hotel and you're all out of ideas."

"I'm never out of ideas," Sam corrected. "I was going to suggest that we circle back the opposite way."

"Actually, I was just testing," Jessica admitted. "I figured that was what you were thinking. Because that's what *I* was thinking. I don't give up easily either. Not when there's something I really want—like finding one of my best friends. I know I didn't act like much of a friend, but I do care about Ellen."

Sam turned away and began walking.

Jessica hurried after him. "Do you hate me?" she asked unhappily.

"I don't hate anybody," Sam answered in a neutral tone. "I just like some people more than others."

"That's an *upbeat spin*," Jessica teased lightly.

"I like you fine, Jessica," Sam said. "I guess I was just disappointed in you."

Jessica glanced down. "I'm pretty disappointed in myself. I guess I'm not too high on your list, huh?"

Sam smiled. A tight, wry smile. "Hey! Don't worry about it. I never stay mad at anybody for long."

They walked along in silence for a while, and Jessica turned her face up. The sky was an odd color. And she could *feel* something brewing in the air. "Sam . . . ," she began uneasily.

He put his hand on her arm and gave it a reassuring

squeeze. "If we don't find her, we'll go back to the hotel, wait until the worst blows over, then start looking again. But we won't give up until we find her."

Jessica smiled. "My thoughts exactly."

Ellen stood in the mouth of the cave, staring up at the sky. "It looks worse than it did before," she remarked nervously. Several yards away, the rocky ground sloped off. "What's over there?" She started toward it to investigate.

Curtis grabbed her arm. "Let's get back inside the cave. Sometimes the wind can take you by surprise. And we do *not* want to get blown over the lip of that ridge." Curtis glanced up at the sky, then smiled mischievously. "It is a killer view, though. You ought to see it at least once. Let's take a quick peek. Hold on tight." Together, they ran the short distance and Curtis yanked her to a stop, inches away from the lip.

Ellen looked over and drew in her breath. "Oh, wow!" It was like looking down into paradise. The ground dropped off twenty-five feet, and she could see a coral reef formation directly below them. Waves broke on the jagged outcroppings sending up towering fountains of white foam. They broke so high Ellen could feel the spray on her face.

Curtis pulled her back in the direction of the cave. "When it's calm, it's a great place to snorkel. Scuba too. But I'm not as good under the water as I am on top of it."

"How do you know so much about this island?" she asked.

Curtis released her hand and slicked his wet hair straight back, looking all around as he walked. "I spent summers here growing up. With my folks. My dad surfs too, and we used to rent a house on the other side of the island. That's the main reason I wanted to come on this trip. I wanted to see this place again."

"Doesn't your family still come for the summer?" Ellen asked.

Curtis studied the ground. "My folks got divorced three years ago. After that, my mom went back to work full-time and my dad got a job in New Hampshire. What can I say? Life got real different." He took a last look around, then ducked into the cave.

Ellen examined his face. The happy-go-lucky expression had gone. His brow had a deep furrow. He looked older all of a sudden. Maybe because he looked so serious. "I know how you feel," she said, following him.

"Yeah, that's what everybody says," Curtis muttered. He turned his attention to his wet suit and began unsnapping the complicated network of black nylon cords that held it in place.

"But I really do know how you feel," Ellen insisted. "You don't understand what happened. And there's nothing you can do about it. But you still don't like it. In some weird way, you feel like it's your fault, even though I bet the first thing your folks said is . . . 'Curtis, this has nothing to do with you and you are in no way responsible.'" She lowered her voice, imitating her dad.

Curtis chuckled and loosened the strap across the belt. "You're right. You *do* know how I feel. Cool."

"I've been there and done that. I'm still doin' it and I still don't like it," Ellen announced.

Curtis nodded. "Tell me about it, man. It just never seems to stop. It's like there's a big cosmic argument that is just *never* ever going to end. Even if they're in different *countries* and not speaking to each other, you feel it bangin' on your ears. That's why the surfing's so important to me. When I'm out there in the barrel, I can't hear anything but the ocean."

Ellen smiled. "Wow, Curtis. That's kind of poetic."

"Whoaaa. Don't make me into something *I'm* not," he said with a laugh. "I'm just a dude who likes to surf. That's all. A lot of people would think I'm a bum." Curtis unzipped one of the pockets of his wet suit and removed a plastic Ziploc bag. "Hold this, will ya?"

"What is it?"

"Cheez Doodles." Curtis unzipped another pocket and fished out another plastic bag. "Coffee-chocolate-creme-center cookies." He unzipped another pocket and produced two small cans of mineral water.

"Sheesh, you're really prepared," Ellen remarked.

"Surfing is hungry work," he explained with a laugh.

He peeled off the heavy rubber suit. Underneath

it, he wore a baggy swimsuit that hung to his knees.

"Aren't you going to be cold?" Ellen asked.

"Probably. But we're going to have to rig up some kind of hammock or something."

"We're in the middle of a hurricane, and you're going to take a nap?"

"I wish." Curtis tapped his foot on the ground, which was now covered with about a half inch of water. "It's gonna get higher. We can't just stand here." He reached into a pocket of the wet suit and produced a knife encased in a sheath. He unsnapped the case, removed the knife, and began picking at the threads that attached the nylon straps to the wet suit.

"What can I do to help?" Ellen asked.

Curtis stretched the suit out on the ground. "Just keep me company," he said happily. "Wow! It's amazing what a guy has to go through to spend some time with Ellen Riteman."

Ellen laughed. "Well you know how it is for us popular—" She broke off abruptly when a scream shattered the air. "What was that?" she gasped.

"Wind," he answered grimly. "The other side of the storm is here."

Jared's hand closed over Lila's and held it tightly. Under any other set of circumstances, having Jared Matthews hold her hand would have been a total thrill. But Lila was too nervous to feel thrilled.

She felt as if the wind might literally pick her up and send her flying.

There was a tearing sound over her head. "Watch it!" Jared exclaimed, yanking her off course just as a heavy branch fell and bounced on the ground, inches from her feet.

Lila swallowed. Those were the first words he had spoken to her since they had left the hotel. They had searched in silence for the last hour, circling the area between the hotel and the dock.

There was a second rumble of thunder, and then water poured from the sky.

Lila's heart drummed inside her chest. She was so frightened, she couldn't even scream. Jared put an arm around her waist and propelled her forward. They were only a few feet from the door to the hotel now. But the wind and churning rain made it hard to see.

Jared guided her past the pool and grabbed the handle of the heavy steel door that led to the stairwell. He pulled it open a couple of inches, and the wind slammed it against the outside wall.

They lurched into the doorway. Jared grabbed the inside handle and pulled with all his might. Lila put her arms around Jared's waist and pulled with him.

The door slammed shut. Lila and Jared tumbled backward and fell against the wall. Jared put his arms around her to keep her from falling. "Are you all right?"

"I'm OK," she said in a small voice.

"Good. Come on. Let's see if the others are back."

Jared started up the staircase, and Lila followed.

They pushed the door open. Lila wondered if a security guard would pounce on them, full of questions. But when they entered the second-floor lobby, the security guards paid no attention.

Lila guessed they were concerned about stopping people from going out. Not coming in.

A few people milled around the area outside the dining room. But most people were inside, sitting at tables and talking in low voices in the dark gloom of the storm.

Lila spotted the others at a table by the window. Mandy waved them over. "Thank goodness you're back. We were getting worried."

"Did anybody find Ellen?" Lila asked.

Jack shook his head. "No. And Mr. DeVille just announced that there's a flash-flood warning. Island Patrol has started evacuating residents. They're bringing a lot of them here and setting up shelter facilities in the third-floor ballroom."

The double doors that led to the kitchen swung open, and Mr. DeVille came hurrying through. He was followed by several hotel staff members carrying piles of tablecloths.

"I guess they're going to use them for blankets," Sam said.

He stopped one of the employees. "Can we get a few of those?" He grabbed a stack, set them on the table, and then opened one up and wrapped it around Jessica's shoulders. "It's cold in here," he said.

"It's colder out there," Kimberly said softly. Her

face crumpled, and she lowered it to her hands.

Peter put his arms around her. "Hey. Come on. We'll find her," he said soothingly.

"It's just so hard to sit here and not be able to do anything," Kimberly sobbed.

"You guys have done everything you can do," Jared said softly.

"No we haven't," Lila said, suddenly sitting up straight. She couldn't believe she hadn't thought of this before. "There's still one thing we haven't tried. Mr. DeVille!" she cried.

Mr. DeVille turned and threw an irritable glance in their direction. He was speaking on a cellular phone.

"I don't think he wants to be interrupted right now," Jared said, frowning at Lila.

"Tough!" Lila shot back. She knew Mr. DeVille was a busy man. But this was an emergency. "Mr. DeVille. I *have* to talk to you."

Mr. DeVille finished his conversation, closed his phone, and strode impatiently toward their group. "What is it now?" he asked brusquely.

"Our friend is still missing," Lila said. She's out there in the storm. And I want you to send out the island Rescue Patrol to find her."

"Mademoiselle, if you must know, Captain Jackson warned me about you girls. He said that you were quarrelsome and overly dramatic. We are in an emergency situation, and I don't have time to humor you. Do I make myself clear?"

Lila set her jaw. It was time to show Mr. DeVille,

Jared Matthews, and everybody else just who was boss. "Mr. DeVille, are you going to contact island Rescue or not?"

"Certainly not."

"OK, then you asked for it." Lila grabbed the cellular phone from Mr. DeVille's hand, opened it up, and started punching numbers.

Mr. DeVille's mouth fell open in outrage. "Give me that," he sputtered. He reached for the phone.

Lila kept dialing. "No," she said simply.

"Lila," Jared said in her ear. "Give him the phone. You're making a spectacle of yourself."

Lila ignored him.

"Who are you calling?" Mr. DeVille demanded.

"My father," she snapped.

"And just who is your father?" Mr. DeVille asked sourly.

"His name is Fowler," Lila answered, her thumb hovering over the last digit of her father's office number.

Mr. DeVille froze, staring at Lila for a moment with his mouth hanging open. "Fowler as in Fowler Enterprises?" he finally asked.

"That's right," Lila confirmed. "And he—"

"Owns the hotel," Mr. DeVille finished, closing his eyes as if he were in pain.

"I didn't want it to come to this," Lila said sadly, "but I'm sure he'd be very disappointed to hear how you let one of his daughter's best friends wander around in a hurricane."

Looking pale, Mr. DeVille held out his hand, and Lila slapped the phone into it.

Mr. DeVille opened his eyes, punched in several numbers and waited. "Lieutenant Marcon? This is Jean-Paul DeVille at the St. Maurice Caribbean Hostess Hotel. We have a problem. A guest appears to be missing. . . ."

Ten

"Curtis!" Ellen cried. "It's filling up like a bathtub."

"Here, braid these and tie the tightest knot you can." He thrust a handful of straps into Ellen's hand and began to work feverishly on the rubber sling he had fashioned from the wet suit.

Water rushed around Ellen's calves. It was cold and full of slimy things that brushed against her skin. She tried not to picture eels, sharks, and poisonous blowfish circling her legs. Her fingers were thick and clumsy in the wet cold, but she braided the strands, tied the ends in a knot . . . another knot . . . and another knot. "I wish I'd paid more attention at those scout meetings," she muttered.

"You're doin' great," Curtis said encouragingly. He took the strands from her, yanked at the two ends to tighten the knots, and looped the braided nylon rope through the rubber sling.

"Wish me luck," he said breezily as he started up the rocky side of the cave wall.

"Good luck," Ellen said automatically.

"No matter what happens to me, don't let anything happened to the Cheez Doodles," he warned.

Ellen patted her shirt pockets to indicate that the plastic bags were safe and sound. "So far so good." She held her breath, watching Curtis grab a stalactite to use as a handhold while he braced his feet on the slippery wall.

He swung out as far as he could and looped the nylon rope around a large boulder with his free hand. The rubber wet suit hung against the wall like a rag. "All right!" he breathed happily.

Ellen stared at the apparatus. Whatever it was supposed to be, it didn't inspire confidence. "I'm beginning to have my doubts about your abilities as a survivalist," she said, watching nervously.

Curtis was concentrating too hard to respond. He tugged at the homemade rope, making sure it was securely placed, then pulled the rubber toward him. Slowly and carefully, he lifted one leg and put it through the rubber loop. "Whooaaa!" He yelled as he lost his handhold.

"Curtis!" Ellen zigzagged crazily beneath him. Would it be better to break his fall if he fell? Or stay safely out of the way and in one piece so she could scream for help?

Curtis swung away from the wall, struggling to

straddle the rubber sling and banging against the boulders.

Ellen screamed, expecting him to come hurtling to the ground.

But he didn't. He swung wildly for a few moments as he struggled into place, and then the next thing Ellen knew, he was sitting up above her as if it were a swing.

"Cool!" he said happily. "It worked."

Ellen quit running in circles and tried to catch her breath. "That's great," she wheezed. "I only have one question."

"What's that?"

"What about me?"

He grinned. "Can you swim?"

"Ha ha," she said dryly.

Curtis moved carefully in the swing.

"What are you doing?" she asked. "And whatever it is, be careful while you do it. I know zip about first aid."

"Ever been to the circus?" he asked, leaning slowly backward until he hung from his knees. He lowered his arms and held out his hands.

"You gotta' be kidding," Ellen said. "You're going to pull me up?"

"No. I want the Cheez Doodles."

"Ha ha," she said again sourly.

"Wow!" he said. "The view from here is totally cool. You're as pretty upside down as you are right side up."

Ellen couldn't help smiling. If she died, at least

she had received one sincere compliment before she cashed out.

She reached up, stood on her tiptoes and put her hands in his. "Do you know what you're doing?" she asked.

"My parents used to send me to circus camp," he explained. "I am totally checked out on the trapeze."

"That's pretty nea . . . whooaaaa!" Ellen broke off with a shriek of surprise as Curtis pulled her off her feet and swung her toward the cave wall.

Jared rested his arm on the table and stared at Lila. He pulled his chair closer to hers so they could talk privately. "Lila. Please tell me straight. Are you who I think you are?"

"If you think I'm the daughter of one of the richest and most powerful men in California, the answer is yes," Lila answered. She looked around the dark room. There was hardly any light at all. If it hadn't been so spooky and scary, it would have been romantic.

"You're not putting on some kind of act to snag me?" Jared asked.

Lila shook her head. "Nope. The acts are over now. I'm rich and spoiled and shallow. Sometimes I'm a bully. And I can be totally insensitive. But I know I hurt Ellen and I feel horrible. I know I hurt you too. What can I say? As usual, I wasn't thinking about anybody but me. But I'm sorry. And if I can put things right, I will."

Jared smiled and squeezed her arm. "You're not as

shallow as you think, Lila. And maybe I'm not either."

"Ms. Fowler."

Lila tore her eyes from Jared's. The other Unicorns and the guys all leaned forward to catch Mr. DeVille's words. Even in the dark, Lila could see that his face was grave. "Ms. Fowler, the beaches are underwater and so are most of the roads. Island Rescue says they will keep an eye out, but there are large parts of the island that are inaccessible right now." He pinched his nose. "At the risk of offending you, I must ask, are you absolutely certain that your friend is not in the hotel?"

"I'm sure," Lila answered, her voice breaking.

Mr. DeVille put his hand on Lila's shoulder. "Then all we can do is hope," he said in a quiet voice. "I'm sorry. Now I must go and set up the ballroom. We have two hundred evacuees arriving downstairs."

Jessica crossed her arms on the table and lay her head down. Her chest and throat were so tight, she could hardly breath.

The room was almost completely dark except for the eerie light from outside. It wasn't really light. It was more like a glare coming off the black sky.

Sam put a comforting hand on her back. "Don't worry," he whispered.

But Jessica couldn't help thinking the worst.

Mandy's hand clenched and unclenched convulsively. The storm outside sounded like a ravening beast. It would have been exciting if she hadn't been sick with worry over Ellen.

A hand rested on hers and then tightened, holding her twitching fingers in place. She looked up and met Jack's gaze. He sat forward slightly and put his other hand over hers. "Try not to worry," he said softly. "It won't help Ellen."

Mandy sighed. She wished it were that easy.

"Push off with your feet," Curtis instructed.

"I'm pushing. I'm pushing," Ellen gasped, reaching out with her feet and pushing off the cave wall.

She and Curtis swung toward the other side of the cave like a pendulum.

The sling creaked ominously.

"It's not going to hold," Ellen said tearfully.

"Yes it will," Curtis said confidently. "Now push off again."

Ellen's feet hit the other cave wall again. She pushed with all her might.

They swung back and forth and back and forth. With each arc, she gained a little more momentum.

"A couple more times and we'll get some real . . ."

"This isn't going to work," Ellen said. "It's not. I can't swing myself up and . . ."

A shrill, earsplitting scream of wind echoed through the cave, followed by a roar. Water came *gushing* in.

Ellen looked down at the raging water. Currents rushed in, and then rushed out. If she fell, she would never be able to get her footing. The water would carry her right out of the cave . . . over the bluff and into the sea.

"Ellen," she heard Curtis shout. "Ellen, you've got to hurry. I'm losing my . . ."

Ellen shoved off the cave wall, let her body flex like a diver, and then used the momentum to swing her feet upward. Curtis let go of her hands and caught her waist.

The next two and half seconds were a blur. Something whacked the side of her head. She bumped her nose. And then somehow, she and Curtis were sitting wedged in the sling. They were sitting side by side.

Or sort of side by side, Ellen thought. She was kind of squashed sideways with one hip cocked against the side of the sling. But she was upright and above the water with Curtis Bowman's arms wrapped around her.

"Bummer," he said.

"What?" she asked in a panicky voice. "What's the matter?"

Curtis nodded toward the water below. A sea of yellow cheese doodles circled around and around before the departing current sucked them down into the water, where they disappeared without a trace.

"I think I've finally had enough pacing," Kimberly announced.

Peter put his arm around her shoulders. "Come on. Let's go in the dining room and sit with the others. At least we can try to keep each other company."

Jack and Mandy sat next to each other, with Jack's hands resting on top of Mandy's. Jessica and Sam had pushed their chairs together, and Jessica sat with her head resting on his shoulder. Lila and Jared weren't touching, but they were looking at each other pretty intensely.

Kimberly sighed. Everything was working out perfectly. At last. But the price was too high. "I don't know about you guys, but I know that I'm not going to be able to live with myself if something happens to Ellen. I'm going to look for her."

Jessica sat up wearily. "I'll go with you."

"You guys can't go out there again," Mandy protested. "It's too dangerous."

"She's right," Peter agreed.

Kimberly tightened her wet ponytail behind her head and started flexing the muscles in her calves. If Lila and Mandy wanted to stay here, she didn't blame them. But she was going out there to find Ellen. "We'll be all right," Kimberly said. "If you guys can just help us get past the guards again."

"I'll go with you," Lila blurted.

"Me too," Mandy said promptly.

Kimberly looked at her friends and suddenly, the room didn't seem so dark anymore. "Cool. Then let's—"

Suddenly, the floor shook, and there was a tremendous explosion. Lila screamed. That was the last thing Kimberly heard before everything went black.

*   *   *

When the window broke, Sam pushed Jessica to the floor. He was shouting something, but she couldn't hear him over the screams and the wind. She flattened herself against the floor and covered her face. She squeezed her eyes closed and thought of her identical twin sister, Elizabeth. All her life, Jessica had turned to Elizabeth for help when she was terrified or in trouble. *Oh, Elizabeth*, she screamed silently. *Wish me good luck! I need it more than I've ever needed it in my life.*

Last year, Lila had gone to a spa where she was massaged with water jets. She closed her eyes and tried to imagine she was at the spa being pounded with vitamin-fortified mineral water instead of lying on the floor of a demolished hotel ballroom in the middle of a hurricane.

She swallowed hard, thinking about her dad. Wishing she had been nicer to him. She wished she had been nicer to *everybody*. Her shoulders shook, and she sobbed loudly. For once, she wasn't embarrassed to cry. Nobody could hear her.

She felt a broad hand rest on her back and give it a comforting pat. Then the hand cupped the back of her head and pushed it gently down so that it was pressed into her arms and hidden from the flying glass and debris.

Mandy couldn't tell if Jack was conscious or not, but she lay as flat as she could and put her arm

over his head. She had failed miserably as a friend
to Ellen. Maybe in the big cosmic picture, she could
make up for it by protecting Jack.

The storm outside sounded to Ellen like some
kind of beast working himself up into the ultimate
feeding frenzy.

This would make a great movie, she reflected, if
only she weren't starring in it.

Ellen trembled from fear. Curtis shivered from
cold. He put both arms around her.

"Don't be scared," he said. "As long as we're
over the water and safe from the wind, the worst
thing that can happen to us is hunger. Shoulda held
on to those snacks myself. Oh, well . . . live and
learn."

Ellen couldn't help laughing. "You know, you
do pretend to be something that you're not."

It was dark in the cave, but Ellen could see
Curtis's eyes sparkle with mischief. "I don't.
Everything I told you is the truth. OK. Look. That circus camp thing? I stretched it a little. It was one
week. And I ran away, which probably makes me the
only little dude in the world who ever ran *away* from
the circus. But I figured you needed that extra shot of
confidence that only a real good lie can give you."

"That's not what I mean, silly," Ellen told him.
"You do pretend to be something you're not. You
pretend to be sort of a dimbulb. But you're way
smarter than the average *surfer dude*."

Curtis laughed. "Uh-oh, man. I'm busted! Oh, well, I guess as long as we're playing spill the beans, I should probably tell you I'm a national honor student."

"Wow!" Ellen suddenly felt inferior. "School's not exactly my favorite subject."

"Sheesh, who's acting like a dimbulb now?" he teased. "But at least you're smarter than your friends. 'Cause you saw past the hair and the accent. And they didn't."

Ellen felt a little encouraged. "Yeah! I did, didn't I?"

"And you're pretty brave too," He added. "'Cause you came out in a bad storm." He tightened his arm around her shoulders.

"That was stupidity. Not bravery," she argued, enjoying the warmth of his arm.

"All bravery is probably stupidity," he commented.

Ellen grinned. "That's pretty poetic too. Promise me something."

"What?"

"If we get out of this alive, please don't fall in love with Mandy Miller. She's into haiku."

He grimaced and reared back like he smelled something nasty. "Eeeeuuuuu."

Ellen giggled. "I was hoping you would say that."

Eleven

Jessica lay on the floor of the dining room, exhausted from shaking. Suddenly, the dining room was silent. The wind had stopped. Jessica lifted her head. The change was so abrupt and dramatic, she wondered if she had fallen asleep.

Very cautiously, she turned her head. The entire, huge dining room was wall to wall with people who had thrown themselves on the floor. Here and there, heads began to pop up. They looked like turtles peering out of their shells.

She turned her head the other way and found herself eyeball to eyeball with Sam.

"You OK?" he asked.

Jessica nodded. "Yeah." She sat up quickly. "I'm OK."

"Kimberly's hurt," Peter said, sitting up too.

Jessica hurried to where Kimberly lay. She moaned and turned over sideways. "Something hit me on the head," she murmured.

"You've got a big goose egg there," Lila said, kneeling beside her. "Don't move until we can get a doctor."

Mr. DeVille was already galvanizing his staff into action. The dining room was a shambles. Several girls, and even guys, burst into tears. And there were lots of cuts and bruises.

"Everyone please stay calm. Medical personnel are on the premises, and we will see that everyone is taken care of," Mr. DeVille shouted.

"Is it over?" someone asked.

"It's over," Mr. DeVille announced.

There was a long silence, and then a cheer went up.

Jessica remained silent. She was glad to be alive. And she was glad the storm was over. But no way did she feel like cheering. Not when their club president and good friend, Ellen Riteman, was still missing in action.

"What do you wanna sing now?" Curtis asked.

Ellen racked her brains. They had sung every TV theme song on the Nostalgia Channel. "Most people would make fun of me for knowing all the words to the *Leave It to Bart* theme song," she said. "It's nice to be with somebody who's not embarrassed to admit they know them too."

"Hey! Watching TV is a totally valid field of intellectual endeavor." Curtis raised a clenched fist. "Tube hounds of the world unite. You have nothing to lose but some brain cells. Hey!" He leaned forward as far as he could. "Look! It's getting light outside."

The wind had died, and light was beginning to illuminate the cave. Within seconds, it was even lighter. Ellen could see that the water below them had receded.

"Is it over?" she asked.

He nodded. "I think so. Darn!"

"Darn?" she repeated. "What are you talking about?"

He grinned. "This is the best date I've ever had. I kinda hate for it to end."

Ellen smiled. Curtis smiled back. He leaned closer and kissed her softly. The sudden and unexpected quiet was the most romantic background music Ellen could have asked for. "Wow!" she said when he drew his head back. "That was, like, totally parabolic, man!"

"Ellen!" Jessica shouted. "Ellen!"

"Ellen, can you hear us?" Jessica heard Mandy's voice in the distance.

"Ellen!" Jack shouted.

Everybody except Kimberly had left the hotel as soon as the all-clear was sounded. Mr. DeVille had alerted Island Rescue, and patrol boats were searching the shoreline.

"Ellen!" Jessica cried.

"Jessica?" a faint voice called out.

Jessica froze. That didn't sound like Mandy. Or Lila.

"Calling all Unicorns," the voice cried.

"Ellen!" Jessica shrieked, running toward the direction of the voice. "Mandy! Lila! I think that's Ellen."

The girls began to run, the guys behind them. Jessica pushed aside branches and limbs, tearing through the jungle. "Ellen! Ellen! Where are you?"

"I'm here," Ellen called out. "I'm . . ."

Jessica swept some vines aside and threw herself into the arms of . . .

"Curtis Bowman!" they all cried in unison.

"Hey, man. Was that storm cool or what?"

Ellen was right behind him. She lifted her hand to high-five Jessica. But Jessica ignored the hand and went right for the hug. But since Mandy and Lila had the same idea at the same time, they wound up tackling Ellen.

They all fell to the ground, giggling.

"Guys!" Ellen protested from the bottom of the pile. "I'm glad to see you too. But this is ridiculous!"

Twelve

"I don't believe it." Jessica looked around the room she and Mandy and Kimberly shared. She shook her head, totally awed. "Our room is totally untouched."

The Unicorns had returned to the hotel and had run upstairs to check out the rooms.

"Our room is fine too," Lila said, coming in the door with Ellen. "No broken windows. No water. We lost no important wardrobe items. Storm damage negligible."

"For us," Mandy reminded them. "A lot of people on this island lost their houses and boats and everything else." She flicked the electric switch. Nothing happened. "I guess the electricity is still out."

"Mr. DeVille said there were no casualties." Jessica reached into the closet for some clean clothes. "And aside from Kimberly's bonk on the head, no real injuries. That's pretty amazing." She handed a pair of pressed linen slacks and a blouse to Ellen.

"We may have some broken hearts," Ellen said quietly. She pressed the slacks and blouse back into Jessica's hands. "I'm sorry. But better living through impersonation is just not for me. I'd rather wear my jeans and sweatshirt."

"Ellen," Jessica began. "We're really, really sorry, but . . ."

Ellen held up her hand. "No. Let me finish. You're not going to like this, but I have to tell you: I really like Curtis, and he likes me. It's going to be a shock to the princes. But I've got to tell them as soon as possible. They need to get on with their lives and quit mooning over me."

Lila shrugged. "But they're not moo—"

Jessica edged her foot over and stepped on Lila's toe as hard as she could.

Lila let out a little yip of pain. Jessica shushed her with a look, then looked over at Mandy.

Mandy was hiding her smile behind a long lock of hair.

Jessica tried to look worried. "Wow, Ellen. Do you think they can hold up? I mean, they've had an awful lot to deal with today."

"I'm not as worried about them as I am about you guys," Ellen replied. "If I break up with the guys, are we still going to be friends?"

"Hmm." Jessica tapped her index finger thoughtfully to her lips. "Well . . ."

Ellen looked worried.

"Well, OK," Jessica said finally. "Right, guys?"

"Right!" Lila and Mandy echoed.

Ellen let out her breath. "OK, then." She stood and squared her shoulders. "This is it. The big breakup. It seems a shame after they were all so worried about me and everything." She opened the door and paused. "But you know, you guys ought to think about dating them yourselves. You don't have to commit right now. But just think about it. No pressure."

"Thanks, Ellen," Jessica said in as serious a tone as she could muster. Ellen left and closed the door softly behind her.

Jessica waited until she was sure the coast was clear and then burst into peals of laughter along with Mandy and Lila.

"Now let's just hope the guys remember their lines," Mandy choked.

"So you see," Ellen said gently, "I've been pretending to be somebody I'm not. And the girl that you've been so crazy about doesn't really exist. Not the way you think she does."

Jack, Jared, Peter, and Sam sat on the soggy wicker sofa in the outdoor lobby while Ellen sat on the edge of a low table facing them.

"There's somebody else—I mean besides all of you," Ellen added. "Curtis Bowman."

"That phony," Jack said angrily, jumping to his feet. "He's taken you from me."

"He's not a phony," Ellen protested. "He really does surf. He's a national champion."

Jared's mouth fell open in shock. "You mean, he really gets out there on a board and . . . "

Ellen nodded.

Peter whistled. "Wow! I can't compete with that."

"And you shouldn't try," Ellen said in a comforting tone. "We need to learn to be ourselves and be satisfied." She leaned forward and squeezed Peter's hand.

"Listen, all of you. I know four really great girls. And they're the real thing. Jared, Lila really is rich and influential. Peter, Kimberly is the athlete of the club. Jack, Mandy wrote that poem. Not me. And Sam, I gotta tell you, Jessica is so enthusiastic, she's like a one-woman pep squad."

The guys all looked at each other.

Jared hung his head, as if deeply hurt.

So did Peter.

Sam pinched the bridge of his nose.

Jack gazed at her. "Ellen, we want you to be happy. And if it's Curtis Bowman you want, then I think I speak for everyone when I say we would never stand between you and happiness."

"He's right," Sam said. He reached out and took Ellen's hand and shook it. "Be happy."

Jared kissed her cheek, and Peter gave her a sad hug.

"Thank you." Ellen smiled at her four princes. They were four really wonderful guys.

Sam still held her hand. He squeezed her fingertips gently. Regretfully. "I guess there's only one
more thing to say."

"What's that, Sam?"

He gazed into her eyes. "Surf's up."

"That's it! That's it!" Curtis paddled along beside her on his own board, shouting encourage-
ment. "You're doin' it. You're doin' it."

Ellen stood on the surfboard with her knees bent
slightly and her arms out. The wave was amazingly
smooth. It was like a magic carpet. She teetered,
working as hard as she could to keep her balance.

Splash!

Ellen went one way, while the board catapulted
out from beneath her feet. The wave broke over her
head with a roar. She stayed under the surface,
moving against the tug until it passed over.

She kicked her feet and swam upward, breaking
the surface and wiping the water from her eyes.

Curtis had retrieved her board and was waiting
for her. "Totally parabolic," he said.

"You're a great teacher!" Ellen commented. "I can't
believe I'm actually standing up on my first day out."

"You're a natural," he told her. "I mean it. I'm
not goofing you to make you feel good. If you prac-
tice, you could be ready to compete in a couple of
years."

Ellen scootched up on the board and lay on her
stomach, resting her chin on her hands. "It would

be nice to be good at something. Something that nobody else is good at."

"It's better to be good at being happy," Curtis commented quietly. He grinned. "You know what really makes me happy?"

"What?"

"That you liked me even when you thought I was a phony. I didn't have to prove myself or anything. You just liked me."

He reached out, and they held hands.

"I still do," she said with a grin. "And I'm beginning to like myself too."

"There's a party in the disco," Kimberly said, struggling with her suitcase.

"What time?" Mandy asked, trying to push her quilted duffel bag through the crowd.

"In an hour," Jessica answered. She was glad to be boarding the ship again. The St. Maurice Caribbean Hostess Hotel had managed to provide breakfast, lunch and hot water for all the Teen Cruise passengers. But they still didn't have electricity, and in Jessica's opinion, life without a blow-dryer was hardly worth living.

A desk was set up on the ship to check the passengers back in. A crewman with a list and clipboard stopped them. "May I have your names, please?"

"Jessica Wakefield, Mandy Miller, Kimberly Haver, and Lila Fowler," Jessica answered.

The crewman checked off their names and smiled.

"Your party has been invited to join Captain Jackson on his private deck to watch the ship's departure," he informed them. "You may each bring a guest."

"All right!" Jessica cheered.

The four girls smacked their hands in the air.

"Let's hurry to our cabins so we can call the guys," Mandy encouraged.

"Where's Ellen?" Jessica asked. "She said she would meet us on the boat."

"She and Curtis wanted to take a last swim before they left," Mandy answered.

"She did know what time we were leaving, didn't she?" Jessica asked in a worried tone as they left the main deck and headed for their cabins. Ellen was always a little spacey. But now that she was in love, she was majorly spacey.

"Sure. Five o'clock." Kimberly looked at her watch. "It's quarter to, now. I hope she's on the boat already. If not . . ."

"She's probably boarding right now," Mandy assured her.

Jessica nodded and shifted her duffel bag to her other shoulder. Mandy was right. Not even Ellen could manage to miss the boat. "Come on. Let's drop our bags and walk around the boat for a while before we go to the captain's deck. We'll leave a note for Ellen to meet us there."

Ellen bobbed happily up and down on the gentle rise of the water. Lying on a surfboard and holding hands with Curtis was the most fun thing she had ever done. And the most romantic. They'd been bobbing and hand-holding for a long time. So far, Curtis wasn't showing any signs of boredom either.

"The boat leaves at five, right?" Curtis asked after a long silence.

"Mmm-hmm," Ellen answered, trailing her free hand in the water.

Curtis stared at her with sleepy eyes. "So, do you think we ought to get going?"

Ellen let go of his hand and looked at her watch. "We've still got loads of time. It's only three thirty."

Curtis took her wrist and studied the watch himself. "I didn't know that brand of watch was waterproof," he said. He stared at it a moment. "Ellen?"

Ellen dipped her mouth into the water and blew some leisurely bubbles. *"Blub . . . blub . . . blub . . . ."*

He put his ear to her watch. "I've got some bad news."

Ellen paused in mid-blub. "What?"

He let go of her wrist. It fell into the water with a *plop.* "Your watch isn't waterproof. Which probably means that's our boat." He pointed out into the distance.

Ellen shielded her eyes and looked out. "Oh, no!" she groaned as she watched the *Caribbean Queen* steam away.

Curtis stuck his tongue down into his lower lip and shrugged. "It could be worse."

Ellen's stomach executed a series of flip-flops.

Her friends were going to kill her. No. First they would kick her out of the club. And then they would kill her. "How could this possibly be any worse?" she demanded.

"We could be someplace where there are no Cheez Doodles," he explained happily.

Ellen giggled. "You have a point there." Sure, she had goofed up again. But so what? As long as she had Curtis, and Curtis had Cheez Doodles, they would survive.

"There's only one thing to do in a case like this," Curtis announced.

"What's that?" Ellen asked.

Curtis began paddling out. "Catch a wave and try not to worry."

Jessica felt very grown-up as she followed the steward through the captain's private dining room and out onto the private deck. Sam walked beside her. Behind them were Mandy and Jack, Peter and Kimberly, and Lila and Jared.

"Welcome back aboard!" Captain Jackson smiled, and Jessica was thrilled to see Anna and Tommy Beardsley, Kickie Crookshank, and Danny Orisman. Finally, they were all going to be able to enjoy being on this gorgeous ship with some totally glamorous kids.

Captain Jackson frowned. "But . . . where is Ms. Riteman?"

"Isn't she here?" Mandy asked.

Captain Jackson shook his head. "No."

"Excuse me." A crewman brushed by Jessica and whispered something to Captain Jackson.

Captain Jackson let out an outraged sputter and hurried to the rail. Another crewman offered him some binoculars. Captain Jackson put them to his eyes and breathed heavily.

Jessica began to get a sinking feeling in her stomach. Captain Jackson looked peeved. And Jessica felt pretty sure it had something to do with the Unicorns.

"I think we have located Ms. Riteman and Mr. Bowman," he said flatly.

Jessica ran to Captain Jackson's side. Lila, Mandy, and Kimberly crowded behind her.

Captain Jackson handed Jessica the binoculars. She looked through them. "Oh, no."

Ellen and Curtis sat on their surfboards, waving good-bye and laughing.

Jessica handed the binoculars to Kimberly. They quickly passed from hand to hand.

"I don't believe it," Mandy sighed.

"Trust Ellen," Kimberly said grumpily.

Lila shook her head and pinched the bridge of her nose.

Captain Jackson chewed the inside of his cheek for a moment. Then he turned toward the girls. "What did you do to her this time?" he asked.

"Nothing!" Jessica insisted.

Captain Jackson looked at her wearily. "I'll tell

you something, ladies. I was a twenty-year naval officer before joining the cruise line. I have piloted aircraft carriers through enemy waters. Rescued men from a sinking ship. Survived ten days in a life raft with no food and water. But ladies, please accept my congratulations. You have succeeded where battalions of hostile soldiers have failed. I can endure no more. I give up. Crew . . ."

Captain Jackson's crewmen snapped to attention. "Yes, sir!"

"At the end of this expedition, I will be resigning as the chief officer of this cruise ship and rejoining the navy. In the meantime . . ." He gazed sternly at Jessica.

"Yes, sir," Jessica said meekly.

Captain Jackson grinned and threw his hat in the air. "Party on!"

"Ms. Fowler. The phone's for you. I believe it's your father."

Lila took the phone from a crewman later that evening. She listened for a few minutes. "I'm fine, Daddy. Yes. Really. Everybody is fine. Except Ellen. She missed the boat. You may have to arrange a helicopter for her. Yes . . . yes . . ."

Lila turned away.

Jessica could tell by the way Lila's shoulders hunched that something was wrong. Moments later, Lila closed the phone and pushed the antenna down.

Jessica hurried over. "Is something wrong?"

"I can't tell," Lila said thoughtfully. "Daddy wanted to make sure I was OK and everything. But he said when I got home, we needed to make some lifestyle changes."

"What does that mean?" Jessica asked.

Lila shrugged. "I don't know. Maybe he's going on some kind of low-fat, high-fiber diet. I guess I'll find out soon enough."

What kind of lifestyle changes will Lila have to make? Find out in THE UNICORN CLUB #18, **Rachel's In, Lila's Out.**

SIGN UP FOR THE SWEET VALLEY HIGH® FAN CLUB!

Hey, girls! Get all the gossip on Sweet Valley High's® most popular teenagers when you join our fantastic Fan Club! As a member, you'll get all of this really cool stuff:

- Membership Card with your own personal Fan Club ID number
- A Sweet Valley High® Secret Treasure Box
- Sweet Valley High® Stationery
- Official Fan Club Pencil (for secret note writing!)
- Three Bookmarks
- A "Members Only" Door Hanger
- Two Skeins of J. & P. Coats® Embroidery Floss with flower barrette instruction leaflet
- Two editions of *The Oracle* newsletter
- Plus exclusive Sweet Valley High® product offers, special savings, contests, and much more!

- -

Be the first to find out what Jessica & Elizabeth Wakefield are up to by joining the Sweet Valley High® Fan Club for the one-year membership fee of only $6.25 each for U.S. residents, $8.25 for Canadian residents (U.S. currency). Includes shipping & handling.

Send a check or money order (do not send cash) made payable to "Sweet Valley High® Fan Club" along with this form to:

SWEET VALLEY HIGH® FAN CLUB, BOX 3919-B, SCHAUMBURG, IL 60168-3919

NAME _____
(Please print clearly)

ADDRESS _____

CITY_____ STATE _____ ZIP_____
(Required)

AGE _____ BIRTHDAY_____ /_____ /_____

Offer good while supplies last. Allow 6-8 weeks after check clearance for delivery. Addresses without ZIP codes cannot be honored. Offer good in USA & Canada only. Void where prohibited by law.
©1993 by Francine Pascal   LCI-1383-123